Introduction.

Welcome to part two of Tens a crowd. Danny McCallister and his family, just after his eldest brother Donnie has been sentenced to a short stay in Barlinnie for some petty theft.

Chapter five (summer days and Dunky's Itch)

Museums and hospitals.

It wasn't exactly the beach on the Riviera or in Barbados but Cessnock Street wasn't a terrible place to spend the summer holiday. It was the last day of school and we had six weeks of no teachers no getting up at seven o'clock no walking a mile in the rain or snow just to spend seven hours waiting to do it again on the way home. We had six weeks of getting up when you felt like it or being woke up by the sun streaming though the bedroom window and we had six weeks of adventure to look forward to, Donnie had six weeks of Barlinnie to look forward to and my Ma was absolutely livid about it with both Donnie and Dunky, but Donnie was safe in Barlinnie Dunky wasn't.

"Ok Ma, I get it, ok just stop hitting me with the brush will you" Dunky was backed into a corner of the hall holding his hands up in front of him trying to ward off blows with a sweeping brush my Ma was swiping at him.

"No you don't bloody get it, you're a half wit, he's got a bloody wean to look after and you get him into this bother, you're a bloody idiot" my Ma shouted at him, punctuating each word with a swipe of the brush.

My Da stepped in and somehow stopped the wild brush strokes without getting hit himself "Enough Maggie, Dunky isn't responsible for what Donald does, they both knew what they were doing was stupid so hell mend them, Annie will be fine, she's here isn't she, she's not going to starve, and anyway Dunky will see her all right for a couple of quid until the older idiot gets out of the jail, it's not the end of the world, it will be like a summer holiday for him, and anyway Annie" he said putting his arm around Annie's shoulder and giving her a slight hug "they say that absence makes the heart grow fonder"

Annie and My Ma just started bubbling again "For god's sake, it's six weeks, it's not life in San Quentin, get a grip of yourselves" my Da said, his sympathy didn't last very long, as usual.

The rest of us had been standing at room doors watching my Ma attacking Dunky and then my Da breaking it up, Darlene was stood at the kitchen door while Charlie and I were stood at our bedroom door, Dunky pushed past Charlie and I and said under his breath "All we need now is fro Donnie's dog to die and we could write a country western song"

I smiled and said "Donnie hasn't got a dog"

Charlie let out a pretend wail and sobbed in an American twang "My Dogless brother's got the Barlinnie prison blues" We thought it was hilarious and so did my Da, Annie and my Ma didn't, Darlene said we were heartless wee tramps and flounced into the kitchen.

"Where are we going tomorrow then Danny" we were lying in bed, it was still light outside and neither of us was tired, tomorrow was the first day of our holiday so it had to be special, Charlie had suggested Kinning park, getting all of our pals together and have a world cup football tournament there.

"I don't know Charlie" I replied the endless possibilities pouring through my mind , that was to be the way it was that summer, we would wake up early, most days before six am, before my Ma and Da even got up for work. We would pack our co-op carrier bag with jam sandwiches or if we were lucky beef paste sandwiches, a packet of rich tea biscuits or co-op custard creams a bottle of alpine pinnappleade and off we went ready to explore and conquer the world. Sometimes if My Ma was in a good mood there would be crisps and sweets left on the kitchen table for us, and it wasn't unknown for my Da Dunky or Donnie (after his release) to slip us fifty pence between us as well.

We roamed all over Glasgow we mostly used the subway as there was a station in our own street, we got a ticket got on and then jumped off wherever we felt like and explored that area, but the place we spent most time by far was the Kelvingrove museum and art gallery, we discovered there was a tunnel going under the river Clyde at Govan, which came out within half a mile of the museum, so whenever it rained

(And it rained a lot in Glasgow) that's where we headed, Kelvingrove Museum.

At first we were treated with great suspicion by the uniformed curators who clearly saw four young boys from a rough background carrying co-op carrier bags, probably up to no good. They would have been justified in their suspicions most of the time, but we loved the place, by the end of that summer we could probably have been employed as tour guides so well did we know the exhibits, and the layout of the place, we knew where to find the Scottish colourists or the Glasgow boys, the renaissance painters or the cubist's.

The natural history part of the museum was our favourite, one day we could be fighting off dinosaurs the next red Indians or Zulu's. There was one occasion when the four of us were gathered underneath a forty foot high T-rex when a museum employee walked back and forth watching us intently and Charlie asked him "What's the matter mister do you think we will try and steal it"

By the end of that summer the same employee was giving us pamphlets to take home on every subject under the sun. Having said that, Searcher did spend the following week coming up with a plane involving wire cutters a horse and cart and giant tarpaulins which would have enabled us, if we wanted, to actually steal the dinosaur, we didn't try it, maybe we should have.

We did everything else you would have expected us to do, we climbed trees and walls, we fell off trees and walls, we cut our hands and arms looking for gooseberries, we had a fair amount of scrapes and bruises, we went swimming in the Summerton road baths, where we actually enjoyed the vending machine hot chocolate more than we enjoyed the swimming, we even, on one occasion went swimming in the White Cart river which runs through the Pollok estate or Pollok country park as it is now known.

We only did it once because I dived in first and got tangled up in some reeds at the bottom of the river and panicked, I thought I was going to drown, Bobby waded in and pulled me to the bank, that was the end of that for us, even Charlie was put off and that takes some doing. A couple of years later Charlie and I saw a news item on Scotland today relating the story of a ten year old boy drowning in almost the exact spot that we had been swimming, we looked at each other and shivered.

We did all of those things and more, we played football, we played street tennis when Wimbledon was on, by tying a washing rope between two lamp posts and calling that our net, we even put a kitchen chair on top of two dustbins for our umpire to sit on, we played kick the can and truth or dare with the girls in the street until it was dark. It was a fantastic summer and on the last but one day of it Searcher got knocked down crossing the road, the car that hit him swerved to avoid me and hit him(Very hard).

"Let's just go home Danny it's pouring and It's freezing, he won't come and look for us he's just gonny stand beside the can until it gets too dark and then he will go home, this is stupid" Charlie whined.

Charlie and I were lying underneath a neighbour's car, watching Bobby who was guarding 'the can'. For anyone who hasn't played kick the can the rules are simple, one person turns their back and counts to one hundred all the other players need to take that opportunity to hide, the guardian of the can then has to find those other people, and anybody he finds could be the next guardian of the can, whilst you didn't want to be found you also had the opportunity, if the guardian of the can was looking elsewhere and had strayed away from the can, to run over and kick the can before being seen and therefore be exempt from being the guardian of the can in the next game, the point being that nobody wanted to be the guardian of the can, well that was how we played, no doubt there are loads of variations.

"Go home then Charlie, just roll out and say to Bobby, it's too wet I'm going home, go on piss off" I advised Charlie.

The most sensible thing for Charlie to do was to follow my instructions, roll out give up the game and go home, but we were young boys, he chose the different option of digging his elbow into my ribs and shouting in a squeaky voice.

"Bobby look under the green Cortina" which as he rolled away was exactly where I was, clutching my ribs, and checking how much damage I had done to my head when I cracked it on the underside of the car trying to grab hold of Charlie the little shit, so Bobby easily spotted where I was and I lost the game.

That's where I should have shrugged my shoulders and accepted it, it was too late for another game anyway, so there was no problem with me saying, "I'm off" and bolting upstairs out of the rain, except for one fact. I was ten years old and my younger brother had humiliated me (In my eyes), so I did what came naturally I chased him.

I chased him up one side of the street and down the other he jumped over fences, I jumped over the same fences in pursuit of him, he ran all the way round parked cars I did the same, he leaned on a car bonnet as I leaned on its boot deciding whether to go left or right in my desperate desire to catch him, and then he broke cover he bolted across the Paisley road, across the heavy traffic on the paisley road, I chased him. There was a pedestrian crossing there, searcher was on it crossing the road he was perfectly safe, he was walking with his head back pouring the crumbs from a packet of cheese and onion down his throat, Charlie ran across the back of a bus I chased him, but as I emerged from the back of the bus there was a car coming straight for me going too fast he swerved and missed hitting me by six inches, what he did hit was the side of the bus, and then the car spun all the way across the Zebra crossing that searcher was on, I could see everything.

It was like a slow motion replay, the car sideswiped the bus and bounced off and started to spin, I could see the driver's face panicking as he desperately turned the steering wheel which was having no effect, Searcher stood motionless in the middle of the crossing, still shaking a bag of crisps into his mouth, striving for the last of the crumbs in the corner of the packet, I wanted to scream, "move, move Searcher there's a fucking car coming"

But despite the slow motion it was all over in a fraction of a second, there was no time to shout and probably no breath in my body to do so anyway. The car had pirouetted all the way round and was now head on to Searcher it hit him on the side of his legs propelling him onto the bonnet, he then bounced off the windscreen straight up in the air and landed with a sickening thud on the boot, he then slid off to the ground.

The world stood still, I could see exhaust fumes from the back of the car frozen in place just above Searcher's head, Charlie stood at the other side of the road also frozen in place a look on his face of awe, like “wow did that really just happen” then the world returned with a bang.

I heard someone screaming “Get an ambulance” and then realised it was me and I was howling like a baby, my legs were shaking I felt faint, I was urging my legs to take me forward to go help, to see what was wrong with my pal, they refused. Or my mind made them refuse, maybe it was self preservation, maybe my mind didn’t like the idea of seeing there was nothing I could do to help, maybe fear intervened for my benefit.

Eventually, by the time I could move, there was a small crowd around him, Mr Ali the shopkeeper and his wife, who was trying to put a rolled up towel under his head, Searchers head not Mr Ali’s. Charlie was kneeling down with his face about four inches from Searchers face and he announced ‘He’s breathing, so he’s not dead”.

Searcher’s was on his back, one of his legs was folded beneath him and it looked as if his foot was facing backwards instead of forwards, Mrs Ali had moved his head to the side, presumably so he didn’t swallow his tongue or choke on his own blood, I learned sometime later, from my Ma, that Mrs Ali was a trained nurse in Karachi where she had came from originally, that’s the most likely reason Searcher didn’t die that night.

Darlene appeared from nowhere and was holding my arm “Is that Searcher, what happened, somebody should move Charlie away, look at him he’s like a wee troll” (I think she meant Ghoul)

“Is he dead, he looks dead, look how white his face is and I don’t think his leg should be like that, he might never become a dancer because of that” she said bizarrely.

I shrugged her off “What are you wittering about when did Searcher ever mention becoming a dancer” I shouted at her in frustration.

“Well, He didn’t but you never know, maybe secretly inside he wanted to, you don’t know everything about everybody you know” she shouted and stormed off trying to get a bit closer to the accident, maybe somebody else would answer her stupid questions for her.

For the rest of that year and the first five months of the following year, Searcher was in a wheelchair, he got out of hospital three times and was re-admitted three times, each time to have his leg re-broken and re-set, when he did eventually get out Bobby pushed him everywhere and when stairs were a problem Bobby carried him in his arms like a baby, or on his back when any distance was involved.

So he didn't die, he didn't become a dancer (I asked him when he was in a hospital bed encased in plaster if he had ever wanted to be a dancer, he looked at me as if I had accused him of being gay he was absolutely positive he had never wanted to be a dancer), but he did walk with a limp for the remainder of his life, and every single time I saw him dragging his left foot, or walking side on to climb stairs, I cried inside, because I knew that it was my fault, maybe he didn't want to become a dancer or a football player or an Olympic athlete but he didn't want to be a cripple either.

So the summer that had been so fantastic had a terrible end which put a downer on the rest of the year, although we did have a fair bit of amusement in December with Searcher and his wheelchair when the snow and ice came, Searcher attached ski's to the wheels, his Da had found a single ski in a midden and Searcher Bobby cut it in half and attach one half to each wheel, we would take him along to Bellahouston park and push him off the steepest hill, if it was particularly icy and slidey one of us would sit on the chair with him and get a hurl. We had to stop it when one of Searchers big sisters happened to see Searcher tumble off the wheelchair halfway down the slope with Charlie sitting on his shoulders, for some reason they didn't want his leg to be reset for a fourth time.

Empty rooms and quiet days.

Christmas that year was as usual quite hectic, the house was still overcrowded, Donnie and Annie were no nearer getting a house, Donnie had lost his job with my Da when he had been in jail, but was now working again as a scaffolder, but off the books, which meant less money and no work in the bad weather, so him and Annie were almost constantly arguing. "How can you go to the pub, we haven't even put any messages in the fridge for a week or gave your Ma any dig money, and you want to take what money we do have and pish it up against the wall, are you really that stupid" we could hear Annie shouting at Donnie,.

My Ma, Charlie and me were in the kitchen along with Paul and baby David, but we would have heard her if we had been a mile away, she was raging. Donnie shouted back "Two quid, is that gonny make any bloody difference, what can we do with two quid, it's Friday night I like a pint on a Friday night, something will turn up next week, gimme two quid and stop your nagging, I'm doing my best, it's not just me that's out of work there's plenty worse off than us" He said defiantly.

"I don't care about anybody else, I want my own house I want you working I want to have a nice Christmas and we canny do any of that if you're in the pub with your Da and your brother can we?" Annie shouted at him.

Donnie replied, missing the point entirely "Dunky doesn't always get in the pub, anyway forget it, I'll stay in this room with you and the wean, maybe somebody will come to the door and offer me a job, I mean it's not as if I could bump into anybody in the pub like Andy McNab or Tommy Watson, I mean they could maybe have work going but you're right I'll stay in this room with you two and hope for the best"

My Da came into the kitchen and handed me three pound notes "Go and give this to Donnie" he said pointing towards Donnie's room with his head.

"Don't you bloody dare" my Ma said grabbing me by the arm before I could do as I was told "Don't interfere like that Davie, let them sort it out for themselves, it wouldn't do him any harm to miss one bloody night at the pub." She added to my Da.

My Da shrugged and said only trying to help, he took the money back off me and then gave me a pound back and said "go and get me ten capstan full strength, hurry up I'm going out in five minutes"

When I returned from the shop my Da was in the close waiting for me, he handed me the three pound notes again and said "Annie will need to let him out of the room sooner or later, even if it's only for a pish, as soon as she does slip him that money and here that's for you and Charlie" he said giving me forty pence and patting my head as he walked away.

It was less than ten minutes later that I was able to slip the money to Donnie, he had emerged from the room to tell me to make a cup of tea for Annie and get him a can of beer from the fridge, even though he knew the four cans in the fridge were Dunky's. When I slipped him the money he grinned and went straight back to his room and a few moments later I heard him shout "I'm not taking this shite all night, I'm going for a walk"

Annie shouted back "What, I didn't say a bloody word to you" when the front door slammed behind him Annie came into the kitchen and said to my Ma "What is it with him, one minute he's being all nicey nicey, I'll get you a cup of tea hen, and the next minute he's shouting he canny take this shite and storming out, when I haven't even said a word, I think he's going doo ally"

My ma looked at me with suspicion written all over her face, I said "Will I make you a cup of tea Annie" Annie came over and cuddled me "Aye son you make me tea, you're a lot better to me than your useless bloody brother" I avoided looking at my Ma and put the kettle on.

My Da Donnie and Dunky came home at eleven o'clock all three were drunk and all three were singing 'Away in a manger', it was three days till Christmas and they were murdering a Christmas carol.

Donnie was first into the kitchen and he grabbed Annie and started singing "We're getting married in the morning"

Annie pushed him away but at least she was laughing "We're already married you half wit"

Donnie had the biggest grin on his face "I know that, I'm not completely stupid, but merry Christmas I've got a job and a house, can you believe it, all because I went to the pub tonight, I got a job and a house so you can shut your face now."

Annie looked at Dunky who seemed to be the least drunk of the three "What's he on about Dunky" she asked.

"He was drinking with Andy McNab who told him he could start right after Christmas, full time, on the books they've got a big job in Middlesbrough that could last at least two years so the jobs his if he wants it, and then Dot's Tony comes in and tells him there's a house going two closes down from him and Dot's already told the boy that owns it that Donnie will take it, and the guy says ok but only if he moves in tomorrow because he doesn't want it lying empty over Christmas and the new year or all the scumbags will have their hogmanay party in it"

Annie's eyes lit up and she hugged Donnie and then said to my Ma "OH Maggie I've got a house at last" but before she let go of Donnie she looked him straight in the eye and said "I thought you were only going for a walk"

He panicked and stammered "Ah, but, ehm, you see"

But she kissed him and said "Lucky you bumped into Andy McNab while you were out walking eh, and lucky you happened to be in the pub telling your Da and Dunky about your new job when Tony turned up, it's just been one bit of luck after another for you tonight hasn't it" Donnie grinned and nodded.

The next day Darlene was ecstatic, "I'm getting my room back and all to myself, at last somewhere to get away from them monsters" Indicating Charlie and I "and somewhere to practice my modelling"

My Da smiled at her and said how can you practice modelling it's just sitting there getting your photo taken"

"No it isnae you know nothing Da, look you need to learn to walk properly, she grabbed one of my schoolbooks from the sideboard and balanced it on her head and with her arms stretched out wide she pranced the length of the living room until the schoolbook wobbled and fell off.

Charlie and my Da burst out laughing when I said "Who would have thought such a wee book could fall off such a big head"

Darlene as usual folded her arms across her chest and stomped out of the room shouting "Ma gonny tell them"

I heard my Ma saying "Oh Darlene, just for once stop your shouting and anyway, you're not getting the room to yourself, I'm moving Pauls cot in with you"

Darlene then had to stomp away in a different direction so ended up stomping into the bathroom and as she did Charlie shouted out, "Don't be all day in there I need a jobby" my Da and me found that really funny even if Darlene didn't.

Donnie and Annie didn't have much so it didn't take long to move all their stuff, we carried everything along the Govan road in carrier bags and boxes, Donnie wasn't remotely amused when I asked him why he couldn't borrow the horse and cart again, it would be handy, in fact he was so not amused he slapped me across the back of the head, really poor sense of humour, I thought.

To move his bed and mattress him and Annie used two prams and just laid the bed and mattress on top, it was too wide for the pavement so they went down the middle of the road, within minutes there was a queue of cars, vans and lorries stuck behind them and some of the drivers were bashing their horns and shouting at them until Donnie ran over and started trying to pull a delivery driver out of a mothers pride van, the guy was hanging on to his steering wheel and screaming like a lassie, funny he didn't seem so much of a wimp when he rolled his window down and shouted "Will somebody get them tramps off the road."

While Donnie was trying to pull the guy out of the van and fight with him, three young boys about ages with Dunky opened the back door of his van and ran away balancing bread trays on top of their heads. "Look Darlene" I said "male models".

"Put the kettle on Danny" We were in Annie's tiny wee kitchen it was Christmas Eve and me and my Ma had been in Govan, my Ma needed messages and she needed me to help carry them.

"It's quite a nice wee house" my Ma said looking around the kitchen and straining to see out of the kitchen to the hall.

"It is Maggie, It's actually alright and it's near enough the shops and Dot's only a couple of closes away, we will need to decorate but we can leave that to after the new year and do it at weekends when Donnie is home" and she started to cry, "We've only just got a house and here he is leaving me already" she sobbed.

"Oh for god's sake Annie he's not leaving you, he's working down in England and will be back up at weekends, he needs to work, you told him that yourself"

"I know but it's not even as if he will be home at weekends it's home once every four weeks for a weekend that's all, I've never stayed on my own Maggie, I think I might move back in with my ma or you" Annie said looking hopefully at my Ma.

"No you bloody won't" she said, though not in a harsh way. "You have wee Mark now and you need to get on with building your own life in your own wee house for Mark and Donnie and for yourself for that matter, you can always go to your Ma's or come to me during the day, but you're not giving up this house, wait and see when he starts sending his wages home and you begin to get this wee house the way you like it, it will be lovely and you'll wonder what all the fuss was about."

Annie wasn't entirely convinced but she did stop crying and looked like she was starting to see that maybe it wouldn't be all that bad. "You can move in here Danny, and at least I won't have to make my own tea" she said smiling.

I was horrified, what about all my pals what about Charlie what about school, no way did I want to leave my house to live in this wee dump. Annie chuckled and said "Calm down Danny I'm only kidding you on, I wouldn't take you away from your mammy".

I hadn't even thought of that, what about my Ma, I couldn't leave my Ma, she needed me. My Ma looked at Annie and said "That's not such a bad idea you know, at least he would be company for you at night"

I was even more horrified, they might actually make me do this, but they both started laughing "Oh Danny you should see the look on your face" Annie said.

Christmas as usual was brilliant. Charlie actually waited until nearly seven o'clock before he woke me up, actually I had been awake for half an hour but didn't want to be first up so I waited for him, well I say waited, I threw some socks and eventually my shoes at him to disturb him into getting up and waking me, Paul was by now almost two years old so when Darlene heard Charlie and I up and about she appeared in the living room with Paul in her arms but as soon as he saw us, and more to the point all the toys he wriggled and cried "Doon, doon, cars". She let him down and he immediately scuttled over to Charlie's pile of presents.

My ma and da arranged our presents individually, all of mine on an armchair, all of Charlie's on the other armchair and Darlene and Pauls at opposite ends of the sofa, there was even a tiny wee bundle in the middle between Darlene's and Paul's that must have been for baby David, it was just some clothes and a wee rattle, but Paul had spotted Charlie's pile first and that was what he wanted, so despite Charlie plaintively pleading "Look over here Paul, look this is all your toys" Paul wanted the Superman and batman figures that Charlie had, or the car transporter with all the shiny new cars on it

He didn't want the cuddly teddy bear or the building blocks that had been laid out for him. Paul loved Charlie, he was his hero, so Charlie didn't know what to do, after a moment's hesitation he said "OK here Paul, you play with batman and I'll play with superman, and we can take some cars each ok pal" and cuddled him, hallelujah Charlie might actually be human after all I thought.

I got mostly games, I got Monopoly and Yahtzee a dice game I really liked, Darlene got a plastic record player and a fancy makeup set, she was over the moon with that, kept going on about being a model, and leaving us tramps behind when she went to London and New York, Charlie asked do you mean London Road and the Barra's?" but even he couldn't spoil her good mood that morning.

Everybody was coming for Christmas dinner, so it would be a full house again, which actually wasn't that unusual. Almost every Sunday since they had moved out Dot and Tony turned up just as the Sunday dinner was being put on the table, my Ma had been threatening Dot for two months that we were all coming to her for Christmas, Dot hadn't risen to it and just said that would be fine but we would have to sit out on the landing stairs because we couldn't all fit in her house unless half of us climbed on to the pulley.

Darlene said "Oh remember you were going to put Mark's cot up with the pulley and just bring him down when he needed fed"

Dot said "No we weren't Darlene that was all in your head"

And I added "I'm surprised there's room for it in her head, what with all the sh.. rubbish that's in it just now" they all laughed but I think maybe at my near miss rather than what I had said.

Donnie and Annie turned up last and it was obvious there was a tension between them, he went into the living room she went straight to the kitchen seeking out my Ma and Dot. "Danny put the kettle on" I heard one of them shout.

"It's Christmas" I said meaning, its Christmas can't you make your own tea for once and let me play with my new games in peace".

Dot replied "Oh so it is Danny, that's lovely, you can put some tinsel round the handle of my cup as well then if that makes it more Christmassy for you, but come and make the tea."

Annie was crying (again) "Maggie he says he's not taking that job, he's not going out the town and leaving me by myself" she whimpered wiping her tears away with a dish towel.

My Ma shook her head and said "You've put him off haven't you with your greeting yesterday that you would go back to your ma's or come back here, what did I tell you, it would be fine once you start getting his wages sent home."

"No Maggie honest, I knew you were right and I said to him that I was kind of looking forward to it, it would be romantic in a funny sort of way, him just coming home every month and we would be dying to see each other instead of being sick of the site of each other, and all of a sudden he gets angry, what are you wanting rid of me for, have you got a fancy man, you have, haven't you, as soon as I'm out the end of this street he'll be up here sniffing about won't he?, I couldn'y believe it Maggie, he just turned, one minute he's telling me everything will be alright and that I will get used to it, and as soon as I agree he starts basically accusing me of being a tart." Annie said breaking down again.

Dot said "What is it with the men in this family, all that jealousy it's ridiculous they ought to grow up"

My Ma arched her eyebrows and said to Dot "So that wasn't jealousy when you tried to stab Tony with a pair of scissors for winching that lassie outside The Jester"

Dot answered "No actually it's different he had actually done something it wasn't just my imagination like it is with men, and anyway, it was a pair of toe nail scissors, which I had in my hand, he's lucky I wasn't making curtains, it wouldn't have been his pride that was hurt it would have been his manhood, if you know what I mean" and she made cutting gestures with her fingers.

Annie tried to smile but couldn't she whimpered again and said "But what can I do Maggie, if I say I want him to stay then he will be on my back because we've got no money and he'll make out that's because I wouldn't let him work, and if I say he needs to go because we need the money, he'll accuse me of all sorts, I canny win whatever I do"

Darlene can move in with you, she's desperate for some peace and quiet away from here, she can move in" my Ma suggested.

"No she canny Ma, you're going back to work with me after the New Year and we need Darlene to watch all the weans, from five in the morning until we get in at eight o'clock, cause my Da leaves for his work at seven and you canny leave the weans with Danny and Charlie, they would burn the bloody house down" Dot said ignoring the fact that I was there and could hear her.

"I don't burn the house down when I'm making the fire every morning or when I'm putting the kettle on twenty times a day " I began angrily, but half way through realised that I was about to talk my away into looking after a two year old and two babies every morning before I went to school, I continued "So I'm not likely to burn it down, but sometimes I need to leave for school before eight o'clock so I couldn't watch them anyway, they didn't notice that I gave no reason for leaving early for school which was just as well as I didn't have one.

My Ma was getting annoyed now I think "Look forget it today Annie, let us enjoy Christmas and the New Year and then we can sort it out one way or another, time to get peeling come on." she said.

Annie looked fed up, but it was probably for the best not to harp on further, my Ma didn't like Christmas being spoiled by anybody, and it wasn't, not really. Annie and Donnie spent most of the day cold with each other in direct contrast with Tony and Dorothy, they were all over each other like a rash, they were like a couple of teenagers, no wait a minute they were a couple of teenagers, sometimes it s easy to forget how young they all were, even Donnie had only turned twenty one the month before.

We had a good Christmas, my Da didn't get too drunk, Darlene spent most of the day her room putting on and taking off makeup, Dot and Annie were in and out of her room trying to help her, but apparently they were too old and didn't really understand skin tone or bone structure. We were all sitting watching a programme about Christmas Carols, from some English church and when the minister was giving a sermon about "We are all God's children" Charlie asked a brilliant question.

He said "Da, if we are all God's children, what's so special about Jesus?"

My Da looked at him and said "Charlie son that's a really good question and I don't know how to answer it, you will need to get your teacher to tell you when you go back to school"

Charlie looked at me and said "You tell me Danny, you know everything"

"I don't know either Charlie, maybe he was just his favourite because he didn't ask stupid questions" I answered, trying to be smart, but it was still a good question.

Happy days and a sore head

New year passed reasonably quietly as well except for one minor incident with Dunky and the Watson's, Dunky had been sniffing around Ina Watson again and two of her brothers had given him a bit of a kicking, it wasn't that bad, he had managed to get up and outrun them before they done any serious damage.

Donnie slagged him off a bit for not being able to beat just two Watson's "Maybe you should have gave Danny or Charlie a shout to help you fight the two wee Watson boys." He said wrestling Dunky to the floor at Hogmanay just after the bells.

Charlie chipped in "I heard it was two of the Watson lassies, not the boys and they slapped him about until he started greeting I want my mammy"

Dunky managed to escape the clutches of Danny and grabbed Charlie and threw him over one shoulder, "Well come on then wee man, out into the hall and let's see what you've got then" he said as Charlie punched him on the back and shouted "Danny"

I pondered going to his aid but couldn't be bothered anyway Donnie grabbed me and said, "Let him fight his own battles Danny, Dunky won't hurt him, he's only having a laugh"

Dunky liked having a laugh with Charlie and me but sometimes what he thought was funny wasn't the same as what we thought was funny, this time but, it was just a carry on and nobody got hurt, this time.

Two days after the New Year my Da came home from the pub and made an announcement to my Ma "I've packed that job on the motorway in, I'm going back to the scaffolding and going to Middlesbrough with Donnie and Andy McNab, so you need to pack me some gear, we're leaving tomorrow."

It made sense there was a lot more money in it and it was a job he loved, the road works had kept a wage coming in but it wasn't his cup of tea. This opportunity meant he would be backing working with all of his mates and out of Glasgow as well, he would be happy and if he was happy we might all get a chance to be happy. I don't think my Da noticed the look of relief on my Ma's face but I did. The situation with Donnie and Annie didn't resolve itself, he wasn't happy about her living on her own, his jealousy wouldn't allow it, but he didn't have a choice and with my Da now on the same job, he basically had to go.

Annie resolved her dilemma by continually telling him it was up to him and refusing to answer when he tried to force her to make the decision for them, because whatever she had said would have been wrong, so an uneasy truce was found. But Darlene overheard him telling Annie that he would have people watching her that would let him know if she was up to anything while he was away. When pressed by Annie he wouldn't reveal who 'people' might be, just that she better be careful what she does because he would find out. "Arsehole" was Dorothy's comment about this, nobody disagreed.

I liked my Da, I enjoyed playing games with him, he had taught me to play chess the year before and was now only giving me a Knight and a castle as a start, and I really did get on ok with him. But even I have to admit when he worked away from home the atmosphere was entirely different around our house. My ma seemed happier, I don't know if that was because she didn't have to deal with his drinking, or his temper or his bad moods. Or whether it was because she had a bit more money coming in, because working away paid more so he sent more home, or maybe a combination of all of that, but she definitely seemed to be happier and consequently so did we all.

Believe it or not, we even got the phone in and my Ma got a posh wee phone table to go with it, with a red velvet seat and fancy back and legs. It was supposed to be so that my Da or Donnie could phone home if the needed to or if my Ma or Annie had to get in touch with my Da or Donnie they could phone the boarding house where they were staying. But as far as I can recall Donnie phoned once a month and that was to say what time they would be home, and I can't remember my Da ever phoning home. Darlene liked it though, it was just a shame the only person she knew with a phone was Mrs Wilson in the next close.

Donnie and my Da came home once a month for a full weekend and when they did it was great for everybody. My Da would come in with a present for everybody, a ball for Charlie or me, chocolates and smelly stuff for my Ma, Darlene usually got a couple of quid slipped to her because there was no chance my Da could pick something she would like. It wasn't just the presents it was the whole sort of holiday atmosphere, on the Saturday morning we would get a big fry up, what my Da called a 'curer' then my Da would spend the afternoon watching the horse racing or the wrestling on the telly.

We usually got a chippy or even a Chinese takeaway on the Saturday night because my Ma and Da would most likely be going out to the pub usually the Camden bar and my Ma did a big Sunday dinner and everybody was there for it, as if it was Christmas and before you knew it Donnie and my Da were away for another month and we would all look forward to the next month. Of course it couldn't last, we weren't meant to be happy all of the time, even some of the time was a major surprise.

"Ma there's that polis Archie brown coming up our close" Darlene said.

She had been sitting at the window in the living room probably trying to get a glimpse of Paddy Wilson, the boy from the next close that she fancied, even if she did deny it. My Ma had caught her on the phone to him at least four times that week and would scream at her that the boy lived in the next close why did she need to phone him, she could walk down the bloody stairs and talk to him for nothing, Darlene's petulant response was that it him that phoned here looking for Dunky. When questioned a couple of days before Dunky said he was a spotty wee prick and he better not be phoning looking for him, he was probably a poof anyway.

When Darlene announced that Archie brown was at our close my Ma's face dropped and she said "I knew it was too good to be true a couple of months of peace was too much to expect, I suppose"

"Maybe he's not coming in here he could be going to somebody else this time" I suggested.

I was at that moment sitting on the floor between Dorothy's feet, she was searching my head for lice, there had been an outbreak of nits and lice at our school and for some crazy reason Dorothy liked looking for them and cracking them on her thumb nails, to such an extent that she would pay me or Charlie twenty pence to let her comb through our hair looking for them so she could kill them, weird but true. As soon as she was satisfied that she had found all the lice, she would take the bone comb and gouge most of my scalp off trying to get the nits out, well that's what it felt like to me. Then lastly she would pour a solution on my head, which smelled a lot like cat piss and everybody could tell you had it on.

If you ask Darlene now she will tell you that she never once in her life had as much as a single nit in her hair, because her hair was clean and lice didn't like clean hair, just manky hair like me and Charlie had. Which means that I have a totally false memory of my Ma holding her over the sink in the bathroom and shouting at her "Hold bloody still Darlene, the more you wriggle about the harder it is to get this bloody lotion through your hair, do you want rid of these nits or do you want to take them to school with you on Monday.

Anyway, there were three loud raps on the door, so obviously Archie Brown wasn't going to someone else's door he was at ours, surprise, surprise.

"What is it this time Archie?" my Ma asked wearily. Both Dunky and Charlie were out so it could have been either of them. Archie Brown wasn't smiling, like he usually was, he normally took great pleasure coming to our door and inflicting misery. He had his hat in his hand and was twisting it round when he asked "Is Davie still out the toon"

"Aye he is, what is it, is this about Davie" my ma asked her voice breaking slightly, she knew this was not going to be good news.

"No, it's your boy Dunky, he's in the Southern General, he's taken a right tanking, they've got him in intensive care, I think you should maybe go down there as soon as you can" Archie Brown said with surprising sensitivity.

Dot was already at our house and she went with us, telephoning her neighbour to pass on a message to tony to let him know here she was. By the time we got to the hospital Tony was standing outside intensive care with Annie. That meant we were all there even the three kids Paul, Mark and wee Tony, who were all in their prams.

"Have you been in Tony, have they told you anything yet?" my Ma asked anxiously.

"No, he hasn't Maggie, we just got here, he was having a fag while we waited for you" Annie answered as she walked over to my Ma and cuddled her.

"Do you think, they should all be here?" Tony asked Dorothy, pointing towards Darlene Charlie and me. "What if it's really bad" he added nervously flicking what was left of his roll up away.

"It's not really bad, my Duncan will be fine Tony" my Ma said with passion in her voice as she pushed past him through the doors marked Casualty, the tears on her face didn't entirely convince she was that sure about what she had said.

It was a very long corridor we had to walk down to get to intensive care and when we got there the two nurses at the front desk looked up in horror at this crowd of people descending on them, all apparently talking at once.

“Shut up the lot of you, I’m looking for my son, Duncan McCallister” my Ma said trying to take control.

“Is he alright?” “Where is he?” “Is he going to be alright” “Is he awake” “Can he talk” “Has he said what happened?” “Does he need to pee in that cardboard bottle” Everybody fired questions at the nurses, I don’t know who asked what, although I’m pretty sure the question about the peeing was Charlie’s.

“Could everybody please keep quiet, there are some very sick people on this ward and they don’t need to listen to this rabble” the older of the two nurses said, “Mrs McCallister if you come with me you can see Duncan for yourself, if the rest of you could please go into that waiting room over there out of the way and please keep the noise down”

As my Ma followed the nurse Dorothy followed her, pushing Tony’s hand away as he tried to hold her back. It was a long ten minutes, we spent it in almost total silence apart from wee Paul who was spinning around the waiting room saying “Bum, willie, shit” over and over again, apparently somebody had been teaching him some swear words, Charlie claimed innocence of course, but every time Paul said those three words he looked at Charlie and giggled, make your own mind up.

My Ma was sobbing, as was Dorothy as she walked by my Ma’s side almost holding her up, Dorothy looked at Annie and shook her head, the look of fear on her face knocked all the wind out of Annie and she started sobbing as well. Tony said “What” he looked at Charlie and me and then whispered in Dot’s ear but we could hear him, “Is he dead?”

Dot shook her head and said through her tears “No, not yet, but they said it’s touch and go he has some swelling on his brain” She broke down even further as did my Ma. Dot took a minute or two to recover and continued “He’s in a coma, the next forty eight hours are critical, but they can’t tell if there’s any brain damage until he wakes up” again she was racked with sobs, this time it took her longer to go on. “They think he was hit in the back of the head with something, more than once, Tony somebody’s done this to my wee brother why would they do that?”

She sat down with a thud on to one of the plastic chairs in the waiting room, sobbing uncontrollably, my Ma stood beside her with Annie holding on to her arm, both of them were also sobbing as was Darlene. Then Paul started wailing clearly frightened by all the women sobbing, Paul's wailing started the two babies crying as well, Charlie and I were staring at Tony, he was the man he should be able to sort this, do something Tony please. He turned and walked out of the waiting room.

Charlie walked across to wee Paul and started consoling him, within seconds Paul had quietened down and Charlie and I then had a pram each bouncing the babies trying to get them to stop crying, by this time my Ma and Dot had got a hold of themselves and my Ma took charge.

" Charlie stop bouncing the pram so hard you will make wee Tony sick, Darlene get wee Mark hen and lift him, I think he needs changed, Dorothy take David off Danny will you please and settle him down" she said getting everybody under control.

"You need to phone my Da" I said, "Him and Donnie need to come home Ma"

We all looked at my Ma, she was white as a sheet, "I know, I know" she said "but when I tell them about this they are going to want to kill somebody, maybe I should wait until we know what happened"

"You canny wait Ma," Dorothy said "what if he takes a turn for the worst" None of us said a word, we all just stared at each other, I was only surprised they didn't all start their wailing again.

My Da was phoned that night, my Ma phoned the boarding house he was staying at but he was out at the pub but he called back at half past ten, him and Donnie would be home the next day, they would get the train first thing in the morning and be home by about one o'clock, my Ma said he sounded angry, very angry.

I went to the hospital with my Ma and Dot, I didn't ask I just sort of tagged along, neither of them objected, Darlene and Annie were left with the kids, Charlie was out playing. We got the subway to Govan cross and walked the rest of the way, it was about eleven o'clock when we got to intensive care and it was a different nurse who spoke to us when we approached the desk.

"Oh you're here to see Duncan McCallister" she looked surprised "Oh dear, I'm afraid that's not possible at the moment"

Dorothy gasped and My Ma asked "What do you mean not possible, they told us there was no visiting times in intensive care, we could come up at any time, why is not possible" I don't think any of us really wanted to hear the answer in case it was what we were thinking.

"I mean, you can't right now he's been taken down for a shower, he should be back in about ten minutes or so" she said standing on her tiptoes trying to see over our heads and down the long corridor, at the same time lifting some paperwork and looking at that.

Dorothy barked "Do you want to stand still hen and explain to me how they can take somebody in a coma for a fuckin shower, are you looking at the right bloody patient"

The nurse let out a nervous half a laugh "No, no, he's not in a coma now, he woke up at about eight o'clock this morning asking for a bottle of Irn Bru or a cup of tea, and if you don't mind me saying some of his comments can be bit inappropriate for a boy of his age" she said once again consulting the paperwork in her hand. "In fact here he is now" she said looking beyond us.

Dunky was being wheeled along the corridor on a trolley, when he was within touching distance my Ma and Dot were all over him crying again. "Ok Ma , I get the message, Dorothy I'm alright get off me will you, I'm ok, aagh apart from this right sore head, have you any aspirin" he said and laughed.

When the nurses had settled him back into his bed we were ushered in and sat around him. "They're moving me down to a general ward later on, they want to keep me in for a couple of days, just to observe me, that will be down to the nurses probably, it will be them that want to observe me most likely" Dunky said wincing every time he moved an inch.

Your Da and Donnie are on the way home they'll be here this afternoon and they won't be happy" my Ma said.

"What do you mean, they won't be happy, what because I'm ok now, do you think I should try and fall out of the bed and put myself back into a coma" Dunky said sarcastically.

“Not because you’re better, because you’re in here at all, who did this to you? My Ma asked “Was it any of they Watson boys”

“Dunky answered but he was lying I knew Dunky and I knew when he was being disingenuous, “I don’t know ma, I was going through that lane at the toll between the Viceroy and the Camden bar and the next thing I know, I’m waking up here with a doctor and a nurse prodding me with needles, I’ve honestly not got a clue what happened, for all I know nobody done this, maybe I fell and banged my head”

“How can you fall and bang the back of your head more than once” I asked “Because the nurse said last night you had been hit on the back of the head more than once”

“I don’t know Columbo, you tell me, maybe my head bounced have you thought of that Lieutenant?” Dunky said frantically making eye contact with me when my Ma or Dot weren’t looking, like he was trying to tell me to shut up as if I was sticking him in it or something, then I thought I understood it must be brain damage, but that couldn’t be right, how could they tell he was dim as a forty watt bulb to start with.

Eventually Dot and my Ma went to the toilet (why do they always have to go together, no matter the circumstance). So I asked him, “have you got brain damage or something, why are you lying, you do know who did this, how can you no tell my Ma, she can tell my Da and he will get it sorted”

“Because my Ma doesn’t need to know, I’ve got a good idea who it was but I’m not certain” Dunky said looking at the back of a nurse who was passing, I couldn’t see anything on her uniform so I don’t know what he was staring at, although her uniform was a bit tight.

“What are you going to say to my Da and Donnie, they’re coming home this afternoon, you’ll need to tell them something, and by the way who do you think it was?, I Think it was probably some of the Watson’s was it?” I asked him when his attention shifted back to me from the nurse.

“Aye it could have been but I’m not sure, and you keep your mouth shut to my Ma as well, she doesn’t need to worry about any of this, if it was the Watson’s me and Donnie will sort they pricks out” he said, but he was still lying I was sure of it.

As I considered how to get the truth out of him Dot and My ma came back from the toilet and settled down on chairs beside Dunky's bed. "So what are the Doctors saying" Dot asked him.

"The one I seen after I woke up says they would send me for another x-ray this morning to see if my brain was still swollen, but it was unlikely since I was compost menthol or something" he said vaguely.

"Compos mentis, it means of sound mind, and if he thinks you are then he's not a very good doctor is he, you should ask for a second opinion." I said laughing at my own joke.

"I've got a second opinion of you, ya wee tube, do you want to hear it" Dunky said wincing as he shifted his position on the bed.

"Danny shut up, so when will they let you out then?" my Ma asked.

"He said a couple of days to see if any swelling was there or if it came back, but I feel brand new, just a bit of a sore head, but I've had worse on a Saturday morning to be honest" Dunky answered again wriggling about and wincing.

"What's the matter with you" Dot asked. "Nothing "Dunky replied.

"Aye there is, what are you wriggling about for" Dot said.

"If you must know my baws are all itchy, ok satisfied" Dunky said wincing again.

Dot smiled and said "I bet that's why you're lying there with your head bashed in, because of your Itchy baws" Dunky chuckled and said "Maybe"

My Da and Donnie arrived in the afternoon as they said they would, once they found out Dunky wasn't dying they said they would catch a train at six o'clock that night which meant they would only lose one days wages and more importantly didn't piss Andy McNab about, they were making good money and didn't want to mess it up. Neither of them actually said anything but it was obvious they thought the women had made a massive fuss over nothing. Dot asked me later If I knew what Donnie and Dunky had been whispering about I just shrugged my shoulders, she obviously didn't believe my innocent look, but I really didn't Dunky was keeping something quiet.

It was actually four days before he got home and all the women in the house were fussing all over him, can I get you this and can I get you that, even Darlene. Charlie spent ages staring at the stitches in the back of his head, once or twice poking a finger in and making Dunky shout and swear, I suppose that signified things were back to normal.

Summer of 72

I was nearly twelve and after this summer I would be going to Bellahouston Academy, I had been taken there by a teacher in May just before the school holidays started and it was huge, the people there must have a map to find their way about. It must have had about a thousand classrooms, it had a football pitch, a rugby pitch, a hockey pitch, a full size running track that ran round the football pitch it had about four gym halls, the changing rooms at the pitches were bigger alone than the whole of Ibrox primary school.

I would also be going their without Charlie, he wasn't happy about that, he thought it was stupid to set age limits for going to secondary schools, he said it should be based on how smart you are. When Darlene suggested that meant he would never go to secondary school at all, he threw her makeup bag out of the living room window, fortunately it landed in the hedge down below and no damage was done, but if I hadn't stood between them and stopped her, we might have found out if Charlie could fly, or at least if that hedge would break his fall they way it had with the makeup bag.

This was another great summer, strangely enough I can't remember having a bad summer until I was over sixteen. But this one good, it didn't rain as much as the previous summer so we didn't spend as much time in the art gallery as last year, but we did discover new parts of Glasgow. One of which was the King George V dock at Govan. We found it by accident one day as we were returning from Partick via the ferry across the Clyde and walking home along Govan Road, when Bobby said "Look at they sand dunes"

I laughed and said "Bobby's finally went crazy, it was only a matter of time, he thinks he's Bobby of Arabia, where's your camel big man"

Bobby replied “Over there look, and Danny don’t give me the hump ok” Not a bad one liner really, for Bobby that is.

We struggled to get on top of a fence that was between us and whatever bobby could see, but Bobby boosted us up on his hands one at a time to see over the fence, and there was indeed mountains of fine golden sand at the side of the dock, they were right below one of the tower cranes that was still in use at that time. We spent the next couple of weeks diving off a platform on that crane into the sand, we never got tired of it, and it was scary particularly when Charlie tried the most dangerous jump, which resulted in him running down the side of one of the piles of sand which was nearest to the edge of the dock.

We all stood holding our breath as he windmilled his arms trying to get his balance back as he hurtled down the slope, he eventually stopped about three feet short of falling into the river Clyde, and turned to us with the largest grin I’ve ever seen and said “Easy, I’m going to do it again” As he had been hurtling down, I was composing an excuse in my mind to my Ma explaining how I had managed to let Charlie drown in the Clyde when we were supposedly playing football at Bellahouston park, I wondered if she would be able to agree with my logic that having five sons was virtually the same as having six, there were so many of us she would hardly notice that one was missing, and anyway wee David and Paul were getting bigger and cheekier by the day, I could teach one of them to be just as much of a little shit as Charlie was.

Fortunately I didn’t have to find out, we went down there the following night and the sand was gone, what was left wasn’t enough to fill a sand pit for a toddler. We filled in this gap in our lives by learning to play golf at the pitch and putt in Bellahouston park, Charlie and I loved it, Bobby wasn’t so keen, co-ordination was never his strong point, Searcher complained that walking too far made his leg hurt, so Bobby would carry him about piggy back until Charlie and I insisted that this was an unfair advantage and he had to stop, Searcher argued the point that there was nothing to stop one of us carrying the other so we ended up playing a mixture of golf and horse polo with me carrying Charlie and Bobby carrying Searcher until we got spotted and thrown out. Charlie reckoned it would have been better and we would have won easily had he been allowed to wear spurs.

The other big news that summer was that Dot and Annie both announced they were pregnant again with both of them being due around March the following year, when they both told my Da that they were pregnant at the same time again, my Da raised his eyebrows to my Ma and asked "What about you?"

My ma said indignantly "Don't be so bloody stupid, I had a hysterectomy after wee David"

"Oh aye so you did" he replied and went back to doing the crossword on the back of his evening Times.

The big school and Dunky's revenge

The big school wasn't as scary as I had thought, the classrooms were all on two floors and once you got used to the whereabouts of the different departments, maths, English, history , science etc, it was a dawdle. I had a slight problem early on with one of the Watson brothers thinking that my dinner ticket money rightfully belonged to him, I fought with him three times because there was no way I was giving up the money but when he beat me for the third time giving me a black eye and a split lip, I told Dunky.

"What happened to you Danny, did Darlene catch you trying on her skirt again" Dunky asked laughing at my black eye.

"No, I want to be as ugly as you when I grow up so I've started hitting my face off a wall every day for an hour" I replied sarcastically.

"Its working" Charlie said, looking up from eating the bowl of cornflakes in front of him.

"No, really wee man, who did that, it looks sore" Dunky asked.

"Ronnie Watson" I answered "I got a good few punches in but he's bigger than me" I didn't like the whiney edge in my voice, but he was actually bigger than me.

"Stand on a chair, and kick his head in" was Charlie's advice.

"I'll kick your head in ya wee tube" was my response.

"I'll have a word with Ronnie Watson for you Danny, I'm sure he will see the error of his ways wee man" Dunky said walking out of the kitchen pausing only to tip up the bowl that Charlie was holding up to his mouth draining the last of the milk and cornflakes from it, Dunky tipping it caused the milk and cornflake dregs to pour down the front of Charlie's shirt, to my great amusement, what wasn't so funny was Charlie throwing his spoon at me and catching me on my sore lip.

"Tell your big brother that my big brothers going to kick his cunt in" Ronnie Watson said to me two days later, I'm sure that's what he said, it was hard to tell because his jaw was swollen and it was hard to hear him properly.

When I responded "Tell him yourself you fanny" and he didn't run after me, I presumed his swollen jaw was down to Dunky and he didn't fancy the same again. I settled into the big school after that and had no more than minor skirmishes with Ronnie Watson or anybody else for that matter, well not until Charlie came up to the big school the following year.

I was in class 1A, which apparently was the top class in first year, they graded the classes on IQ tests we had taken in primary seven. I must have done ok because there was talk of a possible scholarship to Allan Glen School in Pollokshaws but it never came to anything, I don't think we could have afforded all the other things that went with a fee paying school, after all where would I keep my pony in a tenement flat. Being in class 1A did seem to have its advantages though, the pupils in class 1G and 1H spent most of their time making plasticine models and paper chains, at least the teachers tried to teach us.

I made some new friends, through necessity really, neither Searcher nor Bobby would be going to Bellahouston, Searcher was going to Govan high and Bobby was going to a "Special School" apparently he couldn't read or write, I had never noticed, I suppose Searcher must have did all the reading for him. He did the majority of his thinking for him as well if you think about it.

The first of the new friends was Lawrence Kennedy, or Kenny for short , he didn't like Lawrence it was the same name as his father who he hated, mainly because he was a drunk who beat him his sister and his mother frequently but also because he belittled him whenever he could, the first time I saw his father he grabbed Kenny by the hair and dragged him into his house saying “You fuck off midget, Lawrie boy here has some explaining to do, haven’t you spastic boy” and then slammed the door in my face. I think the only reason his parents were still together was that his Da was working offshore on the oil rigs up at Aberdeen so only came home for one week in every six, or maybe they were still together because that’s what people did then stayed together no matter what.

We became friends simply because the desks in English were allocated on an alphabetical basis on the first day of school and he happened to be put beside me for the first week because Kirsty Linton was on holiday. I thought he was rich and posh because his house was on Clifford Street which was comprised of owner occupier houses rather than council houses and before I found out what his Da was like I thought he was very lucky. He had his own room, he only had one older sister and it was possible to be in his house for longer than ten minutes without a dramatic incident occurring, his family appeared to be sane at first glance.

Through Kenny I also became friendly with Colin Cameron , who we nicknamed Coochy, because we went to his granny’s once and she tickled him under one of his many chins and said “Coochy coo, where’s my favourite grandson” so Coochy he became. Coochy lived in Mosspark which was an area I didn’t know very well, it was up behind Bellahouston Park and again I thought it was very posh because people there had cars outside their houses and flowers in the front garden and even swings and chutes in their back gardens, not broken prams and old washing machines.

“Do any of you want an apple” Coochy asked pointing at a huge basket full of apples on a counter next to his kitchen sink, the first time I was in his house.

Both Kenny and I took one and I asked “Why have you got so many apples is that all your family eat”

“No, they’re off the tree in the garden, so for the next few weeks we need to eat as many as we can before they go rotten and need to be thrown away. “ he said pulling aside the curtain and pointing at a tree in his back garden which was heaving with apples.

“Why don’t you sell them then” I asked, obviously two years with Searcher was rubbing off “I bet you could take them to school and sell them for two pence each or something,”

He shrugged his shoulders, “Never thought about it, anyway look at that basket on the counter, it’s probably got about 50 apples in it, so I would have to carry that to school and then go round everybody trying to sell all of them and even if I did manage to sell them all the most I could make would be a pound, why would I bother?”

I was amazed it seemed such a little amount of work for a pound, I could easily fit those apples in my school bag and would probably sell all of them before the first lesson, easiest way to make a pound I’d ever seen. I shrugged my shoulders and said “I suppose so, it’s only a pound” trying for sarcasm, neither of them realised it. His mother came in then and made us some sandwiches and gave us a drink of what was supposed to be coke but it came from a machine thing she had called a ‘Soda Stream’ and it was horrible, Coochy and Kenny loved it or at least they said they did, maybe it was just me being ungrateful, but I did think it was rotten.

As we were leaving his Ma said to me, why don’t you two take a bag of apples with you handing us a couple of carrier bags full of apples, Kenny gave me his on the way home, said none of his family liked apples, strange that because I had seen apples in a fruit bowl in house just a day or two before that. I didn’t care I took them, the only problem was that my Da accused me of stealing them and it took me ages to get him to believe that my new pal had an apple tree in his garden. Darlene said she was gonny have an apple tree in her garden when she was a famous model and a cherry tree and maybe even an orange tree, Charlie told her to get a rowan tree and when she asked why he said so as he could collect the fruit gums when they fell off.

I developed a habit of going either to Kenny’s or Coochy’s after school so kind of started drifting away from Searcher and Bobby, at least I think that’s what happened I hope it wasn’t guilt about what had happened to Searcher that pushed me away. I didn’t stop seeing them it’s just that the tranquillity of either of my new friend’s houses seemed much more attractive than the mania of Searcher’s house or mine, so the actual time spent in or around Cessnock diminished considerably, this didn't go unnoticed.

"Danny come in here son" my Ma shouted from the kitchen. I had just arrived home and had thrown my school bag on to my bed and went straight into the living room to see what was on the telly, it was eight o'clock on a Friday night there must be something on. I went in to the kitchen to see what my Ma wanted, probably tea.

"Where have you been" she asked.

"Nowhere" I responded.

"You can't have been nowhere, Danny, everybody is somewhere, where did you go when you got out of school, four hours ago" she said looking at the clock on the kitchen wall, the wooden one with the little cuckoo in it, which Charlie and I had got her at Christmas, the cuckoo still popped out every hour, but it didn't have a head anymore, Charlie knocked it off with a spud gun.

I couldn't think where this interrogation was going "I went to Coochy's with Kenny and then went to Kenny's before I came home, how?" I asked wondering what I had done wrong.

"I went to Coochy's" Dunky repeated in a stupid voice as he stood behind my Ma buttering toast. "Oh Coochy you're my best pal, can I have some more apples please" he said in a voice intended to be like Oliver Twist I think. Then Charlie joined in "Ooh Kenny can I borrow your fur coat mine is at the cleaners" in what I supposed was also meant to be a posh voice

I wasn't getting this had something happened, had I done something wrong? "What's the matter with yous two are you jealous, I'll ask Coochy if you can get some Tomatoes from his Da's greenhouse if you want or I'll ask Kenny if he's got any old clothes that would fit you" I felt a bit angry, what had my new friends done to either of these two.

"Don't show off Danny" my Da said walking into the kitchen "they don't need anything off your wee rich pals" Oh good it was my Da's weekend home, he can have a go as well then I thought.

"What wee rich pal's is that, I think maybe yous have all been reading the beano too much, having an apple tree in your garden doesn't make you Lord Snooty" I said vehemently.

"And maybe you want to wait to you're the size of Desperate Dan before you talk to me like that" my Da said and slapped me on the back of my head with his paper. It was on the tip of my tongue to tell him desperate Dan was the Dandy not the Beano, but I thought better of it.

"You have been spending a lot of time with your pals Danny you never seem to be in the house anymore, I mean what have you had to eat tonight, you're not even coming home for your dinner most nights" my Ma said gently.

"Mrs Cameron gave us all some shepherd's pie and chips" I said almost crying "and what's the matter with my going to my pals house it's not as if I can bring them to this dump is it" I said walking out of the kitchen in a mood with tears threatening to brim over, not realising that I had unintentionally hurt all of them, but then I was twelve years old, a tiny step away from the hormonally driven monster that is a teenager. Nobody made a big deal of my strop but it would be a long time before I was old enough to realise that even the strongest families have fragile points, I didn't have any problem with who we were or where we came from or how we lived but did my new friends shine a light on us that we didn't want to see, I hope not, I liked us the way we were.

It was a one day wonder, nobody mentioned it again but as you know by now in my family problems get shouted about for a day and then are put away to fester for a while before coming back with a bang.

It was the end of October Halloween and bonfire night were coming along, I was still just about young enough to go out for my Halloween and also do penny for the guy. Despite Charlie's suggestion that I should get a top hat and dress up as lord snooty, or Dunky's suggestion that I should dress up as desperate Dan, I actually got Annie to lend me a white nightgown and I went out as wee willie winkie, Charlie put a white sheet on cut out two holes for his eyes and went out as Casper. My Da had actually brought us home two Frankenstein masks but how could we both have dressed up as the same thing, they got put aside to be used on our guy later.

When we did go out we did ok loads of monkey nuts, tangerines and apples a few sweeties and about a pound each, not a bad night, we would probably have got round more doors if we didn't have to drag wee Paul with us, Darlene had dyed one of his old babygro's red and stuck some cardboard horns onto a headband so he looked like the devil, to be fair but she did make him a wee cardboard fork out of sellotaped together toilet rolls centres and it was quite good, until Paul wacked Charlie over the head with it and it fell apart, and then when he lost his headband and horns he just looked like a wee jelly baby, which everybody thought was really cute.

The best money was to be made with a penny for the guy, Charlie and I stood outside the Clachan bar which was quite near our house, this was a prized location and we regularly had to fight the two youngest Watson brothers for it, you could make up to a fiver there on a Friday or Saturday night. So Bonfire night and Halloween were two good earners, Charlie and I used to push an old pram about with our guy in it, our guy was an old pair of trousers and a jumper stuffed with newspapers or old rags and either an old bust ball with a face drawn on it or a Halloween mask of Frankenstein or something.

Searcher was his own guy, he used to put old trousers and wellies on and a big baggy jumper and pull the jumper up over his head and put an old ball on top of his head, then Bobby would just push him from pub to pub in his old wheelchair. He did this for ages until Bobby went for a pish in a close and two wee boys tried to push his wheelchair out in front of a car on the Paisley road about twenty yards from where he got knocked down the year before, Searcher jumped off the wheelchair and started punching the wee boys about the head, he told me later they shit themselves, he didn't mean they got scared they literally shit themselves, he said he could smell it off them.

Bonfire night was always good there used to be a huge bonfire in just about every tenement back court, ours was always the biggest, we would prepare for it from September onwards any wood we seen anywhere was collected and put in our back court, and pile up against the factory wall ready for November the fifth. We had a whole ceremony and a set of rules about actually putting a match to the bonfire. It couldn't be lit until eight o'clock at the earliest, it had to be lit by whoever had collected the most wood that year, it couldn't be lit until somebody had climbed right to the top and put a guy on it, and other more stupid things like no mattresses because last year a straw mattress burst and because it was windy there was burning bits of straw everywhere, floating in peoples windows and everything, eventually the fire brigade came and put our fire out, that was a disaster.

The fire got lit, by Bobby at ten past eight, it was a cold clear night which was a change because it had been raining nonstop for days, Searcher was with us, technically he was a visitor because he didn't stay in any of the closes which surrounded our back court he lived across the street, but he said their bonfire looked shit and anyway all his sisters were over there and they were doing his head in. It took Bobby a while to get the fire started most of the wood was saturated with rainwater, but eventually he got it lit and after about twenty minutes it was a tower of dancing leaping fire, sparks from pieces wood with nails left in were flying everywhere.

About an hour later the fire had now burned off all the light wood and cardboard and had collapsed in on itself and was now devouring the doors and old sideboards and really thick scaffolding planks at its core, most years people from the surrounding houses would appear with old broken furniture or piles of yellow newspapers and magazines to throw on the fire and get rid of, it would be kept going in this manner until after midnight. The four of us sat on the concrete roof of the midden and stared into the fire, searcher took four cigarettes out of his pocket and handed us one each, he lit his with a practised ease cupping it in his hand protecting it from a nonexistent wind.

Charlie looked at his and then looked at me, I gave him the slightest shrug of my shoulders, he glanced up to our kitchen window, my Ma Darlene and Dot had appeared there periodically, it was also a Sunday night so my Da could appear back from the pub as well, him and Donnie were getting the first train at five in the morning. I looked at Charlie to see what he intended to do, he put the cigarette in his mouth tasted it and then handed it back to Searcher “That tastes like shit” he never again, to my knowledge tried a cigarette.

I lit mine took two puffs and discarded it “It does taste like shit Charlie”. Bobby smoked his to the butt mimicking every gesture Searcher made with his. Before the end of the night Charlie went upstairs and within minutes came down with a bag of potatoes and a roll of kitchen foil. I wrapped the potatoes individually in foil and pushed them into the centre of the fire with a long stick where we left them for about fifteen minutes, when we pulled them back out and gingerly unwrapped them what we could see was a burnt lump of charcoal, I peeled back some of the black skin exposing a centre of potato which I then ate, it tasted half raw and half burnt, we all declared them the best food we had ever tasted and wolfed them down. Gordon Ramsay eat your heart out.

Despite our strongest pleading and begging and downright disobedience we eventually got dragged up to our house just after midnight. Annie was sitting at the kitchen table deep in conversation with my Ma and Darlene. “So any way both of his legs and both of his arms are broke, and they think there could be some spinal damage as well, he is in a hell of a state, Irene’s beside herself, she’s in bits, it’s a sin so it is” Annie said shaking her head, she didn’t look particularly upset at what appeared to be devastating news.

“Irene who” I asked full of curiosity.

“You’re a right nosey wee bugger, it’s none of your business” Darlene replied.

Annie looked at me and said “My sister Irene, her man Ian has had a hell of a doing tonight, in his own house as well, Irene says she was out at a bonfire with the weans and when she came back he was lying in the loaby floor greeting and covered with blood and a sledge hammer handle he kept under his bed was lying right beside him., go on put the tea on Danny”

“Aye ok, but who was it that done it, do the polis know about it” I asked going to the sink and filling the kettle. As I stood filling the kettle you could still see the glow from what remained of the fire, I could also see a reflection from behind me someone was stood just outside the kitchen door listening.

Annie continued, with a little excitement in her voice Annie liked a bit of drama, "He wouldn't tell them, he said whoever it was wore Halloween masks and he couldn't see their faces, but the polis told Irene they were sure he knew who had done it and just wouldn'y tell them, he was in a hell of a state but maybe he was just in shock"

My Ma said "In a way I suppose it couldn't happen to a better person, he's not exactly slow at lifting his hand to your Irene is he, he'll no find it so easy giving her a black eye with two broken arms will he" and she giggled the looked a bit embarrassed.

"No I suppose not" said Annie "The shoe will be on the other foot for a while"

"If he's got two broken legs he won't be wearing shoes at all for a while, will he?" I said, they all laughed.

Charlie asked what masks the guys that did it had been wearing, Annie laughed and said "The polis found two Frankenstein masks in the close, whoever they were they were a couple of monsters." Everybody laughed again but I had a sudden thought, and just as it was forming in my mind the person who was standing at the kitchen door listening came in, it was Dunky and then I knew, and he seen the realisation on my face and said "Frankenstein eh, felt a bit like him myself when I had all the stitches in my head" and winked at me.

It never came out in public I mean the police never found out, who had battered Ian, the only person in our house who didn't eventually know who did it was my Ma, my suspicions were actually wrong it hadn't been Dunky it had been Donnie and my Da, Dunky had been told to go and stand in the Viceroy Bar all night just in case the polis came looking for him. Obviously this was in retaliation for what happened to Dunky, it came out eventually that sleeping with Irene at the wedding wasn't the only time Dunky was with her he had been doing it on and off ever since. Irene's husband Ian had lain in wait for Dunky and set about him from behind with the same sledge hammer handle that was found by his side, If he had challenged Dunky and just had a fight with him no retaliation would have ever happened but what kind of man sneaks up on a sixteen year old boy and almost kills him by attacking him from behind, he was a coward and deserved everything he got, he didn't have spinal damage and recovered fully after a few months, such a pity really.

Annie was disgusted by her sister and fell out with her for years because she knew fine well what age Dunky was after the wedding so she had no excuse. My Ma never found out about that either, but it was probably just as well my ma could be worse than my Da when it came to protecting her weans. Annie's brother in law should have been happy it was my Da that visited him on bonfire night and not my Ma.

Chapter six, (Weans, more weans and Letters from abroad)

Christmas had came and went in a flash this year it was just as good as ever but no proposals or revelations about pregnancies like last year. Dot and Tony had settled down into their house quite nicely and she was a good six months gone with her second, she was just as cranky this time as she had been the first time, Darlene reckoned Dot was going to be a fat grumpy old woman before she was twenty one, Dot said that at least she was going to reach twenty one which was more than could be said for Darlene. Donnie and Annie had also settled into their house quite nicely, Donnie still wasn't over his paranoia when he was working away, he would often tell Annie that he wouldn't be home until late Friday night when he was due home for the weekend and then arrive early in the afternoon, always with the excuse that the train was a lot faster than he thought.

Annie threatened to buy a tailors dummy and tuck it under the blankets on her bed one of these days, just to see what Donnie would do when he came home and seen it, she was persuaded that Donnie wasn't exactly well known for his sense of humour, and it might not be as funny as she thought it would be, she seen the light. Dunky had two or three lassies on the go as usual, the latest was a lassie from Govan, I hadn't met her yet but Darlene described her as hatchet faced and a cow, it takes all sorts I suppose. I have been basically going my own way and doing my own thing, I more or less split my time between Mosspark and Cessnock, there's a lot less people who want to fight with me in Mosspark, probably because Charlie's never been there.

Talking about Charlie, he had been suspended from primary school, over allegations that he had been bullying a young boy in primary three and taking his dinner money off him, it turned out not to be the whole truth, the young boy had sought Charlie out and offered him his dinner money on the understanding that Charlie would stop Stephen Watson from bullying the young boy, Charlie achieved this by telling Stephen Watson that the young boy was his cousin and that he would poke Stephens eyes out if he even looked at the boy again. Charlie had been accepting this dinner money for months and it only came to light when a teacher seen the wee boy lifting a bit of chocolate off the playground and eating it, she might not have thought anything of it if he hadn't looked so happy to find it.

Paul was walking and talking like a right wee man now, Wee David was sitting up on his own just about, everything was hunky dory really, but what were the chances of that lasting for long.

"But who is it that's coming Ma, is it your cousin or your auntie, I don't know what you mean" Darlene said, she was sat at the kitchen table with my Ma, me and Charlie, we were all having our dinner, Paul was sat with us in his high chair but he had fell asleep with spaghetti hoops all over his face and down his front.

"Your Auntie Phyllis is my Ma's Sister, so Colleen that's coming over for the New Year is her Son's wife, so I think that makes her my first cousin through marriage, or that might mean my second cousin, I don't bloody know, just call her your cousin Colleen, what bloody difference does it make anyway, she's coming tonight and staying until the fourth of January" my Ma said as usual getting exasperated with Darlene's incessant questions.

"How long is it since you've seen her and do you wish you lived in Ireland instead of your ma coming here before you were born" Darlene persisted.

"I've never met Colleen she only married Phyllis's boy Graham last year and the last time I seen your auntie Phyllis was at my wedding and that's many years ago, she must have been nearly seventy then, I'm surprised she's still living." She paused "And to answer your question, when I was wee I used to wonder what it would have been like to grow up in Ireland, I canny imagine it would have been harder than it was to grow up in Partick, with everybody calling you a wee catholic bastard all the time, my Ma used to tell me stories about picking totties in the fields and how everybody had a tan in the summer because they all worked out in the fields all the time, and she missed having warm milk straight from the cow in the mornings and she always said the eggs in Glasgow were never as fresh as she had when she picked them out of the hen house." She paused again a faraway look in her eyes, she didn't often talk about when she was wee never mind about when her ma was wee, so we were all silent waiting to hear more.

"Och but that disnae get the dishes done does it, thinking about the past, come on Darlene you wash and Danny can dry, Charlie you can just watch less chance of broken plates then eh?" she said going to stand up.

"No Ma don't get up , tell us a bit more about what it was like for your ma and Da in Ireland, I wish we lived in Ireland" Darlene implored, I sometimes think Darlene just wanted to live absolutely anywhere but here, and most of the time I think she did live elsewhere in her head that is.

"Five minutes, I'll have a fag and a cup of tea" She smiles at me "And I'll tell you a wee story about my Ma and da and then dishes done and everything squared up for Colleen arriving and then I'm sure she can tell you more" she said smiling, I don't think it was a hardship for her to reminisce about her parents. I poured us all tea and put the biscuit tin in the middle of the table, I asked my ma if she wanted me to butter her a piece, because one of her favourite snacks with a cup of tea was a piece and butter with a chocolate digestive biscuit in it, don't ask me why, but since one of my favourites is a slice of bread with tomato ketchup all over it, I've got no room to talk about strange snacks, mine's is a little stranger in that I don't like ketchup on my food, any food.

"My Granny and Granda were both born in Cavan, which is the big town in County Cavan which is in Southern Ireland but right on the border with Northern Ireland, they met when they were at school and were together for the rest of their days, and she only died the year you were born Danny so she lived to a good age, you would be too wee to remember Darlene but she absolutely loved you, she said you were the spitting image of her Ma and her sister Phyllis, she would never put you down, I always had to end up dragging her away from you when I wanted you to have a sleep, but whenever she came by there was always a wee matinee jacket or hat and bootees or something in her bag that she had knitted for you, I think it was probably her that gave you the big head, she was forever telling you how beautiful you were going to be and how you would be a right heartbreaker when you grew up, you were only about three when she died, but you used to walk about saying, where's my good granny, your Da's ma never found that as funny as I did." My ma chuckled.

"Cheek, I've not got a big head" Darlene protested. Charlie and I guffawed at that.

"Well maybe not a big head but she did spoil you, but anyway, what I was going to tell you was what happened when my Granda asked my Granny to get married, her Da was dead against it because my Granda was a bit of a scoundrel as a boy, like you Charlie" she touched Charlie's chin and smiled at him " he was always up to some mischief or another, there was no harm in him, he just enjoyed himself a bit too much for some people, he was always the same until the day he died, anyway your Granny's Da said over his dead body would they get married and that was that, my granny's ma wasn't so bothered she could see that Charlie, I mean my Granda wasn't a bad lad so she turned a blind eye whenever he came calling."

She took a sip of tea gathered her thoughts and continued "Your Granda was determined to bring him round so he asked your granny's Ma what would be the one thing he could do that would change her husband's mind, she said she would think about it and let him know, anyway a week or two later, he asked her again and she said she wasn't sure but she thought her man's problem with your Granda was that he thought he was a lazy good for nothing boy and he would turn out to be a lazy good for nothing man, so your Granda would have to think of something to do to convince him that he wasn't" My ma smiled as she recalled the story, "So for months after that your Granda would try and look busy whenever he seen your Granny's Da passing but he never seemed to notice and then, bingo he heard in the local pub that your granny's Da was having real bother in his bottom field with not enough water for the cow, so he would have liked to dig a well out there but he wasn't as young as he used to be" My Ma stopped and stood up.

"What are you doing" I asked "you're right in the middle of the story"

"I need to pee" she said "It must be thinking of all that water running down the well it's made me need the toilet"

By the time she came back there was another cup of tea in front of her and Darlene was sitting giving wee David his bottle. "So where was I, aye your Granda decided this was the very thing, he would dig the best well in Cavan, in fact the best well in Ireland and show the old bugger he wasn't lazy, it took him eight months, he dug it all by hand it was thirty feet deep, by the time it was finished, and it was stone lined all the way down, with a wee roof and a winding rope and a bucket, it might actually have been the best well in Ireland after all. He went and seen your great Granda and dragged him out to the well and showed him it and the old man was impressed and agreed to let him marry your granny" Charlie and I laughed and then we heard a noise behind us.

Dunky said "That's Maggie McCallister sitting at the table there and stood aside to let a woman with long blonde hair and a beautiful happy smile into the kitchen behind him, before any of us could say anything she said "Don't be laughing yet boys, that's not the end of the story, I heard the well was forty foot deep, and when your great Granda was doing the speech at his only daughter's wedding, he said that he had always liked your Granda and would have let him marry your Granny a year earlier, but your great Granny had come up with a terrific idea to get a well dug in that bastard bottom field" We all burst out laughing and that's how we met Colleen.

We all liked her from the very first second we met her, she took less than ten minutes to put any lascivious thoughts out of Dunky's mind and within twenty minutes she had a fan in Darlene, in fact she had a stalker in Darlene. Darlene followed her everywhere "Can I get you that Colleen" do you want some of this Colleen" "can I make you tea colleen" it would have made you sick, especially making the tea, what was I supposed to do with all my spare time if Darlene was making the tea. I'm sure Darlene actually had a wee Irish brogue by the time the bells came two days later.

We had a particularly good time at the bells, Colleen was the centre of attention for the whole street, they were all coming in and saying "Oh what a beautiful lassie, and such a lovely accent as well, and she seems so down to earth" My Da Donnie and Dunky all stood around her glaring at any man who dared approach within ten feet, and she ended up dancing with Darlene most of the night because any time a man even thought about dancing with her he would look at them three and change his mind pronto. She heard that I had learned the dashing white sergeant for the school dance and asked me to show her it, I went crimson and couldn't move my feet with embarrassment and ended up saying I need a pee and running out of the room, when I came back in I stayed out of her way, I wasn't going to go through that again. The best laugh of the night was when Dunky was dancing with Darlene and he twirled her around and caught her and then stopped and said, "Wait a minute Darlene, when did you get them?"

"Where did I get what, my earrings" she said flicking her hair back and showing her earrings.

"No them" he said grabbing at her chest "They boobies, where did they come from they weren't there this morning." She started screaming and struggling "Ma, goony tell him, Ma he's hurting me, Ma get him off me"

When Dunky eventually let her go he turned round triumphantly and said "Ta ra" like a magician pulling a rabbit from a hat, and he held his hands up and in each was a white sports sock.

"I hate you, I hate you" Darlene screamed and grabbed the socks, "and gimme them, I need them I'm going to the dancing tomorrow" and ran out of the room, I hope she never heard all the laughing but she probably did.

The next day at about tea time my Ma Dot and Darlene were sitting at the kitchen table with Colleen, you can guess what I was doing, you guessed right I was making them tea.

"Well the thing is I need to go and see my ma's uncle in Maryhill, I could have went and stayed with them but my Auntie Phyllis told me what a great laugh you lot would be and she convinced me to come here, but I need to go and see my ma's uncle to see what they want to do about Phyllis" Colleen said looking round at my Ma.

Darlene sat opposite Colleen, with her elbows on the table and her chin her hands hanging on every word she said, if Colleen wasn't careful Darlene would stretch over and lick her face in a minute. My Ma asked "what do you mean, what are they gonny do with Aunt Phyllis what's up with her, is she ok"

Colleen smiled and said "Oh absolutely, she's never been better, in her nineties but as fit as a butchers dog, so she is. No Graham and me are going to America for a year, another one of my uncles has a business in California and we are going over to see if we like it and we might stay there if we do" Darlene started to actually slabber, she might end up eating this lassie if we didn't watch her.

"Oh my god how great would that be California" Darlene squeaked "That's where the beach boys come from, oh my god"

Colleen giggled with her and said "I know, I'm right looking forward to it, but the reason I'm in Glasgow is to see if any of the Maryhill mob would want to come over and live with Phyllis until we get back, we don't know how she'll manage she has only got Graham and me and we do all her shopping and everything there's still some other family over there but she could do with somebody moving in really"

Darlene screamed “I’ll do it” wee David burst out greeting in his pram and my Ma nearly jumped out of her skin.

“For Christ’s sake Darlene you near frightened the life out of me, you’ll do what?” my Ma asked.

“I’ll move to Ireland and stay with Auntie Phyllis, and look after the poor old soul” Darlene said almost jumping up to start packing.

“Don’t be stupid” my Ma said “you hardly know the woman and anyway what about School, and what about this lot, how will I manage, I need you here”

Darlene’s face fell faster than a stone down a well, she stood up and walked out of the kitchen, she didn’t stamp her feet or slam the kitchen door or slam her room door, the only thing we heard was her throwing herself on to her bed.

Dot looked at my ma and shrugged her shoulders , Colleen said “Oh Margaret I’m so sorry, I never thought, I really didn’t I wasn’t trying to get Darlene to say that, Oh I feel so bad, after you have all been so good to me, I’ll talk to her Oh I’m really sorry.

“No don’t be sorry Colleen, Darlene has these fancy ideas all the time, I’m just surprised she didn’t want you to take her to California with you, I’ll have a word with her in the morning when she calms down, I’ll tell her she’s too young” my Ma said sighing.

“She’s fifteen ma she leaves school in the summer, she’s not too young and if she really wants to do it, it’s not very fair saying she canny because she has to watch our weans is it. Anyway it’s only for half an hour in the morning we really need them watched and Danny can do that can’t you Danny?” Dot said surprisingly sticking up for Darlene or maybe she just wanted rid of her for a year.

Not wanting to let Colleen down, I nodded and let myself in for a year of greeting weans in the morning. My Ma pondered it for a minute or two and said "Danny go and tell her I want her"

I knocked on her room door, not because of manners because she had scratched my face the last time I went in without chapping and she was singing into her mirror with her hairbrush.

"What do you want, piss off" I heard her, but only just, I pushed the door open and went in.

"My Ma wants you, you've to come ben to the kitchen" I said quietly.

"No she doesn't want me, she wants you and she wants Charlie, she loves Charlie and she wants the two weans, but she doesn't want me or she doesn't want me to be happy anyway so piss off and tell her I'm staying in here until I decide where I'm going to run away to, I might even run away to California if she's not careful so piss off, go away." She sobbed and started beating her pillow.

"Ok will I tell her you don't want to go to Ireland then? Will I tell her you've changed your mind because you're a greetin faced wean, she says you can go if you want ya eejit" I said unable to keep the fact that I was happy for her out of my voice.

She sat straight up "You're kidding me on, Danny if you're kidding me on I'll never talk to you again for your whole life, or even my whole life" she said daring to believe, that perhaps I wasn't kidding and her dream was about to become reality.

"Darlene that's not even a real threat, that would suit me perfectly if you never talk to me again, you talk the biggest lot of shite I've ever heard anyway, why don't you threaten to phone me every night from Ireland, that would be a real threat." I said smiling.

She jumped up, I'm sure she actually touched the ceiling and screamed "I'm getting out of here Danny boy, I'm going to live in Ireland" when she landed she grabbed me and kissed me.

I said "It looks like it, but mind it might be cold in Ireland you should pack extra socks" she looked confused until I nodded towards her chest and then she went red grinned and hugged me.

The next couple of days passed in a whirlwind of packing unpacking and packing again, the end result being that Darlene wanted to take every single thing she owned right down to the dolls she had had since she was a baby, my Ma and Dot eventually got her down to the essentials, which constituted two large suitcases and two small suitcases. For somebody who was hyper by nature Darlene was wired to the moon for those two days, I don't think she slept at all, I reckon she was asking Colleen questions at the rate of about one hundred per hour, she didn't walk, she bounced everywhere, if she had been a puppy she would have worn out her tail. I think it's fair to say she was both happy and excited.

On the morning she left, we all gathered at the living room window and watched as she walked down the subway steps, dragging a large suitcase and carrying a small one, as did Dunky who was going as far as Central station with her, and then it was just her and Colleen, they were getting the train to Stranraer and then the ferry to Belfast and the another train to Cavan in Ireland where she would be staying. It was a big deal none of us had ever been away from home for any length of time, this was an unprecedented adventure and a wrench for all of us, it also meant a complete imbalance in the house, it would be my Ma and all boys.

The night before she left she was talking to Dot and telling her she would write to her and phone her whenever she could, I asked her to write to me as well. I had caught some of her excitement and wanted to be involved in whatever capacity I could, I told her it was for a school project, it wasn't, it was to satisfy my nosiness, I suppose. I promised to write to her every week with all the gossip about the family the street her pals anything that happened with school, Coronation Street and whatever else I thought she might like to know. But I like to think those letters made it possible for everyone to get through that year, for Darlene to cope with the bouts of loneliness she had and for my Ma to see that her baby girl was not just surviving but blooming.

My Ma wasn't supposed to see the letters that Darlene wrote to Dot, but I think she did, I don't think Dot could have avoided showing her them, I never seen them until Dot showed me them many years later, I didn't have a clue, it put her letters to me in a much clearer perspective. Darlene wasn't the most literary of people, she could read and write perfectly adequately, her spelling let her down sometimes and her tendency to get long words completely wrong was both endearing and funny. I've decided I can't really tell you about her letters and do them justice it would be much better to read them for yourself, so here we go, I haven't included them all just enough for you to get a flavour.

6/1/1973

Hello Danny

It's Darlene here, your sister, this is the first chance I've had to write to you I got here the day before yesterday and it's been mental, I can hardly understaun what my Auntie Phyllis is saying hoff the time and she says I talk too fast, what does that mean talk too fast too fast for what, she's really really auld she looks about a hunner and ten or something.

I'll tell you somethin for nothing ,I'm never going on a boat ever again. I was sick everywhere their was an auld man sitting right next to me and I was sick on his shoes, I didnae know where to look, his wife says it was ok and she would clean it up, with the look on her face but, you would think somebody had asked her to lick it up, It wisnae my fault but, it was my Ma's fault saying this morning, oh you better eat up and have a big breakfast Darlene you don't know when you might get something to eat again. Well I hope she's happy that poor man got my cornflakes all over his shoes and some carrots, I don't even remember when I last ate carrots.

The train wasn't any better than the boat it was bouncing all over the place as well, I was putrifried I thought it was going to crash or something. But it could have been worse Colleen told me she flew in an aeroplane once from Belfast to London(She's been to London) and the flatulence was that bad she thought they were going to crash into the Irish sea.

Cavan is the very last stop on the train track after that there's nowhere else so this must be the back of beyond, I told you it would be, you said it might be a big place , it isnae. Govan is much much bigger there's more pubs than shops here. Padraig, my auntie Phylises nieces son which I think makes him my ma's second cousin which makes him my third or fourth cousin, I don't know, says it's really busy at the weekend because hardly anybody lives in the town they all live outside the town and just come in at the weekend really, Padraigs seventeen, he says I will fit in foine here, thats what he sounds like foine this and foine that. He keeps saying ach sure it will be foine, everthings foine with him I think

He said I look older than 15 and when I told him I was going to be a model in Paris and new York, he said no wonder I was a right foine looking girl, I think he might be a patter mershant. Are wee Paul and Davie ok, I'm missing them already, I know thats daft because I never want to watch them when I'm there but I miss my cuddles from wee Paul. Is Dot getting fatter yet, I know I've only been away a few days but the way she was eating at the new year you would think she was eating for four rather than two, and she's not exactly Twiggy anyway is she, don't tell her I said that, in fact forget I said that at all, I might rub that out later, she'll batter me when she sees me if she thinks I said she was fat, even though she is.

For such a wee toon there's a lot of big fancy buildings here, the toon hall and the courthouse are absolutely lovely, from the front the toon hall actually looks like the Whitehouse in America you know where the president lives. My auntie Phyliss used to be the cleaner there, in the toon hall I mean no the Whitehouse in America ha ha.

I know what your thinking why am I looking at buildings, but you said you wanted to know what the place is like for your project so I'm telling you. thats just about all their is here, there's the cathedral as well and then the town centre which is one street and then hardly anything else and everything's a lot cleaner than Glasgow and smells better, but that's probably because you and Charlie urny here ha ha.

I'm gonny try and write once a week or every two weeks, and gonny tell my Ma that I'm alright and I will phone in an emergency, Auntie Phyliss hasn't got a phone but Padraig says there's one in the pub that everybody uses and nobody would listen if I wanted to use that, except for Mrs O Brien who sits right next to the phone but she wouldn'y say anything to anybody if I told her it was a private conversion.

Is Dunky still seeing that skinny lassie from Govan the hard faced one, I didny like her the first time I seen her, which was when she was sneaking out of our living room the morning after boxing day, she looks like a right tramp, I hope he gets rid of her, and tell him to stop drinking as much as he does as well it's getting like he's drunk all the time.Tell Charlie to stay out of my stuff, if there's anything missing when I come home I'll do him in, and that goes for you as well.

Tell Annie and Donnie that I'm missing wee mark and them as well, I feel as if I've been away for months and it's only been two days but it's brilliant I'm gonny be so happy here, I bet I talk all Irish by the time I come home, I'll be saying that's a foine thing to do Charlie, you're very bold. Right I'm going to make auntie Phyliss something to eat so I will write again soon, I've got my own room it's a bit damp and cold but it's ok really, it was snowing here last week and there's still a bit of it lying about Padraig says he will build me a snowman later.

Right cheerio and you better write me back straight away you promised me you would, you better.

Love

Darlene

7/1/1973

Hello Dorothy

You were right my sore belly was my period, I came on at the Central station and I was heavy all the way here, I wasn't due do you think my Ma was right and it was just worry and excitenment about coming here, anyway this is the first chance I've got to write. I know you said there would be boys here that might be patter mershants but I didn't think it would be full of them, I met a nice boy straight away, Padraig his name is he's taller than Dunky and he's got long dark hair and a dreamy smile, and he was, I'm trying to think of the right word, he was charming but I didnae think that was for my benefit, he's like that with everybody as far as I can see, he's seventeen, he's got a wee brother as well who's sixteen, his names Micheal, he's a bit strange really quiet and staring at me all the time a wee bit creepy really. You can ask danny what the place is like I described it in my letter to him, I'm no gonny write to you about the river and the buildings and everything i'll tell danny all that for his project, I'll just tell you the good stuff.

I hope wee Tony is better and it doesn't turn out to be that hoopla cough and it's just a wee cold he's got, and by the way you were wrong I'm not on the first train back hame. It is all right here so far, my Auntie Phyliss sleeps a lot and she dribbles down her chin when she's sleeping she sits on an old chair in front of the fire all day getting me to make tea, I feel like Danny ha ha, I've not met everybody yet she says they will all troop in sooner or later because their no too busy in the fields with the snow and that, did I tell you it had been snowing, well it has.

It's really really dark here at night, there's no street lights, when I opened my bedroom curtains last night I couldn't see my hand in front of my face, it was scary, and I think there might be mice in the kitchen as well, I seen some mouse shite, Auntie Phyliss says it was probably feild mice they come in to the hoose for the winter, well thay can piss off out again I hate them.

I've not got much more to tell you it can be a wee bit boring sometimes when nobody's visiting and Phyliss is sleeping, I can tidy up and that but it disney take long, and I forgot to tell you they've not got a washing machine, I have to do all the washing in the sink, there isn't even a laundrimart near hear, it's big blocks of green bubonic soap and a wash board it's like something from the old days. I think I'll be making my nickers last a few days, talking about knickers I washed phylisses this morning, my god they were enormas, they were like a parashoot, if I'm cauld again the night

I'm just gonny throw a pair on the bed as an extra blanket, I don't know how I'm supposed to dry her clothes she says put them outside but it's freezing can you imagine trying to struggle in through the wee back door with a pair of her knickers frozen solid, you coodny do it.

I will write again next week, I'm missing everybody, has Jimmy Simpson been phoning looking for me, let me know.

Love

Darlene

Ps, I hope your no putting on too much weight.

21/1/1973

Hello Danny

I got your letter, Dunky must be drunk all the time if he's gonny keep going out with hatchet face, tell him I said he's mental he should stay away from her she's trouble and that's terrible about Charlie getting suspended again he's gonny end up in borstal if he's not careful. Its good your doing all right and school and don't listen to Dunky and Charlie your wee pals aren't homosapiens, just because theyer not rough like them Disney mean their poofs, you hang about with who you want it's nothing to do with them.

I don't think Dot would let Tony hit her she must have got that black eye from banging in to a door, she's seven months pregnant, my Da woud kill Tony if he hit her, it must have been an accident right enough, if she says it was it must have been she would kill him if he hit her pregnant or no, do you think he hit her, i'm gonny phone her, is wee Paul a lot bigger I'm really missing him the most and wee david, it's good that he's nearly walking but a shame he keeps banging his head, thats probably why Charlie is the way he is, banging his head too much when he was wee. Annie will end up leaving Donnie if he disney stop his jealousy how can she be messing about when she's nearly due she must be the size of an elephant by now, don't tell her I said that.

I went a walk along the river with Padraig and Micheal a few days ago, you would love it Danny they said that people have got gold out of that river before but I don't beleve them, auntie Phyliss says its true that years and years ago people did get gold and made jewellery out of it, she said she used to have a ring but she lost it in a feild when she was as young as me, and she said when she was my age she was already married with a wean, can you imagine that.

Padraig,s got two wee brothers michael and thomas, tommy is just about your age, he says you should come over in the summer, I keep telling him about you, how clever you are and he's the same, always sitting with his face in a book, he was reading a book about a big whale last week boaby dick or something, who would be interested in a whale, except Tony, don't tell dot I said that, never mind I'll rub it out before i post it.. Auntie phyliss isny too well I think maybe its a flew, she's being a bit sick and that. I've made pals with a lassie called shivawn but she spells her name Siobhan, she works in the pub at the corner she's really nice I think Padraig fancies her.

Oh my god, I nearly forget to tell you there was a huge fire in an orphanige on the main street here, thirty five wee lassies were killed and an old woman that worked there, it was terible there were weans as young as four and there was even a set of twins who were twelve years old the same as you, it must have been horrible. This was in 1943, I seen the grave its beautiful and its got all their names listed on it, it would break your heart, I asked my auntie phyliss about it she said she could remember it like yesterday. The fire was supposed to have started in a laundry room, probably because of an electric fawlt, nobody notice until about two in the morning, when one of the lassies from the dormitory on the top floor told the head nun about it, and there were people out on the street who noticed all the smoke coming out as well, they tried to kick the front door in to get in, a wee lassie did let them in but they didney know the place and couldn't find there way about in all the smoke. Somebody said laterthat all the weans had been moved upstairs into one dormitory by the nuns, people say that all they weans could have been evacuated before the fire got worse but the nuns persuaded some of the local men to try and put out the fire instead, two men went in and tried to put the fire out, a John kennedy and John McNally, auntie phylis says the fire was too big by then and Mcnally collapsed and would have died if kennedy hadn't pulled him out, I suppose that made kennedy a hero.

By this time it was too late to get the weans out the stairs must have been on fire, the local fire brigaide arrived but they didney have a long enough ladder so they were telling the lassies to jump, it was two floors up it was higher than our window, I would have been terified some of them did and got broken bones but lived, but most of the lassies were screaming they were to scared, my auntie phylis says she was there and everybody was screaming and greetin it was the worst thing she ever saw, she said a man called mattie Hand turned up with a big ladder but it was too late, one man did go up the ladder Louis blessing she said he was called and he goat another five lassies out but he coodny save any more and the rest of them died. She said there was a big scandal about it after and there was an enquiery that said it was mostly the fire brigades fault but a lot of local people think it was the nuns to blame and that it was covered up to protect the catholic church from blame. The nuns were called the poor Clares, it was the poor weans I feel sorry for, Shivawn showed me the grave down the cemetery, I was greetin the whole day after it, I canny stop thinking about all they lassies.

I don't want to write any more today I'm sorry, I'll write again soon tell everybody I miss them.

Lots of love

Darlene

29/1/73

Hello Dot

Thanks for the letter it cheered me up a bit, I suppose danny must have told you about the orphanage, I canny stop greetin every time I pass that cemetry. But it was funny how you got your black eye I'm glad you told me about that cause I thought if it was tony that hit you my da would have killed him, and maybe you will watch what your doing with wee tony's rattle in future. I canny believe Dunky let that hatchet face stay with him in my room, what is he thinking about he's far too good looking for her. Is it just nine weeks to your due I hope your not getting too big, but never mind you lost most of your flab after wee Tony, well maybe no most of it but a good bit of it, well some of it anyway, I'm sure you will do the same again.

I am sure Padraig fancies me, he took me a walk down by the river last week, do you know ther's gold in this river, no never mind, anyway he took me for a walk and he kept trying to hold my hand and he tried to kiss me a couple of times but his wee brother Micheal turned up and spoiled it, I don't like him he appears from naewhere sometimes and frightens the shit out of me, he's like a a wee ghost or a gull or something, creepy wee basterd.

But then shivawn who works in the pub, have I told you about shivawn, she spells her name funny and she works in the pub, anyway shivawn that works in the pub told me that Padraig wants to go out with her, she said that he's asked her to go to the pictures so do you think she's trying to make me jealous or is Paddy just at it with both of us, I think she might be a bit jealus cause shes a bit fat and I told her I was going to be a model in London, so if she spoils things with paddy and me I might have to scratch her eyes out, only kidding she's alright really, she sneaked some vodka out of the pub the other night and me and her got a bit tipsy, don't tell my ma.

My aunty phyliss has been no well shes been shitting her bed nearly every night and she's even started shitting them big knickers of hers, she canny get into the tin bath that theyve got, did I tell you they don't have an inside toilet or bathroom like us, anyway she canny get in the bath and am having to wash her down in the bed, its horrible am up to ma elbows in shite some mornings, I didny know it wood be like this, I thought I wood be making her a bit of tea and helping her with her messages and that no cleaning up her shite, but theres nobody else to do it, paddys ma is in a wheelchair and his da barely says two words to anybody. Am scunered with it, I asked her if she should see the doctor and she says she canny afford it, they need to pay to see the doctor here that canny be right can it, she cood be really no well or anything. I went and told Paddys ma about it she says she will talk to his da and see if theres any money for a doctor or if theres anything else he can do.

Apart from that everything else is hungry dory, I knew that wee prick Jimmy Simpson would be chasing after Ina Watson the minute I left for Ireland well hell mend him he'll probably end up with a dose of crabs or goninherhear or something shes a manky bitch.

Write to me again and tell my ma thanks for that tenner it will come in handy, Dunky sent me a fiver and so did Donnie so I'm rich just now.

I'll write back after you write to me.

Lots of love

Darlene.

3/3/73

Hello Danny

Thanks for your letter I'm sorry it's taken me two weeks to write back i've been really busy, the weather wisny too bad in February so I have been helping Padraigs family out in the feilds most days, theyr planting seed potatoes and onion sets, they say it's a bit early but it seems warm enough, I seen a wee baby cow being born last week, its called a calf, it was yucky at first but then after it was born the mammy cow stood up and licked all the blood and stuff off the baby and it was lovely, that padraigs terrible he said that wee calf will make about two hundred lovely burgers, I might become a vegetable eater, who could kill that wee cow and eat it, Micheal says we could call it Darlene after me, I slapped him, imagine him looking in the feild and saying look everybody theres Darlene the wee cow, basterd that he is.

Thats good that Charlie hisny been in any bother for a while and that Dunky has fell out with hatchet face maybe him being drunk all the time isny always a bad thing, and I don't believe your growing a moustache your pulling my leg your no immature enough to grow a moustache yet. Dorothy told me how she got the black eye she was playing with wee Tonys rattle that one I got her its on like an elastic string for across the pram and it bounced up and hit her on the face, I knew she wouldn't let Tony lift his hands to her, and neither would I let anybody do anything to me.

It's really good that you write to me danny I get a wee bit fed up some times, its quite hard work here as well sometimes, and I look forward to you telling me how wee paul and david are getting on and even what Charlie's up to I suppose, I miss yous all, I'll never shout at yous again when I come hame. I have talked to another few of the people that seen the orphanage fire, they mostly say the same thing, that it was the nuns fault and they got away with it, Shivawn even pointed out the two men that went into the fire theyr still alive, their old now but still alive, I don't think much else has happened here that I can tell you about for your project but one of the old men was telling me that Cavan was the site of a mass grave during what he called the famine a hunner and odd years ago he said thousans of people died maybe you could go to the library and find out about it, it seems like they don't like to talk about it round here, no wonder but.

Right I need to tell you somthing I don't want you to tell anybody, my aunty Phyliss hasn't been well and you need to pay for a doctor here and they canny afford it so I had twenty pound that my ma and the boys sent me so I spent that on a doctor, well he charged twelve pound so I've still got some left .The doctor said to me at first its old age, I laffed and said she must be about a hunner and ten of course its old age but what can you do for her, and he said nothing, that I'm doing all the right things keeping her fed and clean and keeping her warm, he says if she lasts into the summer he would be surprised, he said that right in front of her she just laffed at him and said she wood see him in the grun before her, theyr all mental, don't tell my ma I spent that money on a doctor, Padraigs da said I was wasting my money the old biddy has outlived her welcome anyway, he was half drunk when he said it but I think he meant it, he's wors than oor da when he's drunk.

I'm still pals with Shivawn it's mostly her thats been showing me roon everywear and she says she'll try and find out things you can put in your project for you, I still talk to Paddy and Micheal sumtimes but not all the time cause ther busy in the feilds a lot just now as well.

Anyway I.ll write soon see you later

Lots of love

Darlene.

25/3/73

Hello Dorothy

I canny believe it a wee lassie gonny tell Annie thanks for phoning the pub here and leaving a message Shivawn came right round and told me, we got drunk later to celebrate some mare free vodka, happy days. It was magic to talk to you on the phone as well but you sounded a wee bit tired and I wisny talking Irish you were making that up, i hope you wirny I would like to talk irish maybe I,ll try having a mixed accent Irish and Glesga I would like that, Im gonny try it when I come hame.

Anyway, a wee lassie and your calling her Daisy thats really lovely, I canny believe I'm missing out on seeing my wee neice, she'll be nearly walkin and talkin before I come hame, well no really but you know what I mean, I'm dying to see her, I bet she looks just like me I hope she hasn't get Tony's big ugly nose that wood be a shame, how can I be missing her so much when I've no even met her yet, I canny wait.

By the way that Padraig's a basterd, Shivawn says he was kissing her and trying to get his haun up her skirt behind the pub last night, he was in their boozing all night and waited for her to finish and grabbed her, she said that she pushed him away but I think she only said that cause she knows I fancy him, I think he's a sheep in wolfs clothes cause the night before he had his hand up my skirt and I was letting him as well, I feel bad about it now cause of what shivawn said he did to her, but what if she's just makin it up I don't know who to believe when I pull him up, he just gives a me a load of barney I think he's kissed the barney stone when he was wee. I don't think shivawns making it up because whenever she can she brings vodka from the pub and we get a bit drunk, and she widny do that if she was lying to me wood she.

And I think Micheal was spyin on me when I had a bath last week, I waited till it was late and I filled the bath on the kitchen floor, I shut the curtains but when I got in the bath a draft must have opened them just a wee bit, cause I,m sure I seen a shadow crossing the windy and I jumped out of the bath and put a towel roon me, then I pulled the front door open cause whoever it was

was gaun towards the front, Micheal was on the other side of the street just staunin their with his hauns in his pockets, I'm sure it was him, I told Paddy, he just laffed and told me I've a foine body and not to be shy with it, I told you he was a patter mershant.

Aunty phylis is getting a bit better which is a surprise cause the doctor said she wouldn't last to the summer, I think shes trying to prove him wrong out of badness, she still shitting herself and the bed sumtimes but she hardly eats anything now so theres no as much shit if you know what I mean, she seems to be getting a wee bit doolally shes called me colleen a couple of times and Helen a couple of times as well, I don't know who Helen is but it looks like Phylis didny like her she keeps saying things like Helen come her you wee basterd. She's struggling to eat now as well, sumtimes i need to feed her its not any diferent from feeding wee tony or mark she puts her hand up and pushes the spoon away the way they do and spits more down the front of her than she swallows, I really like it here but I didny think I would end up looking after a twelve stone hunner year old wean.

This is just a short letter cause I know youll be dead tired with all your paternal duties now that youv got two weans, so tell everybody I'm missing them especialy wee tony, not big tony I'm not missing him throwing me about and tell Annie I hope she has a wee lassie as well how good would that be two wee nieces to come hame to, I can dress them up like wee dolls, I'll turn them into wee fashin models like me eventually. Gonny tell me in your next letter what I should do about paddy, I do like him but what if shivawns tellin the truth, I'm not sure what to think.

Lots of love

Darlene

22/4/73

Danny

I canny phone Dorothy I canny what would I say, what would anybody say when somebodys baby dies, gonny tell her how much I love her I canny talk to her Danny I just keep greetin whenever I phone her all I do is scream and greet I canny talk to her gonny tell her I canny talk to her Danny please, I never even seen daisy how can she be gone, I never even met her, she never even goat to meet me, oh my god, I want to come hame, I know I coudny get hame in time for the funeral but I want to come hame noo I hate it here, tell my ma I want to come hame I need to see Dorothy danny somebody needs to come and get me please I need to come hame, oh please please please gonny somebody come and get me, please danny.

23/4/73

Hello Danny

I think I might have posted a letter to you last night, I was really drunk but shivawn says I did, if I said anything bad gonny throw it away, I canny believe what happened to wee daisy, I know its been nearly a week since it happened but I still canny believe it, I never even met her Danny, there I've started greeting again. I was greeting last night and screaming at shivawn that I want to come hame, but I don't cause I canny face seeing Dot, danny it would be too hard, how is she, gonny you phone me when you get this letter, hows my Ma I bet she's thinking about her first wean as well, oh god I'm sort of glad I'm not there, no I'm not really, oh I don't know what to say. Shivawns been great shes been looking after me when I've been drunk, don't tell my ma, Paddy and Micheal are staying well away from me, they know whats good for them, I was shouting at them as well when I was drunk last week.

Gonny tell Annie I've sent her a wee scarf and hat set for her wee lassie Mrs O brien knitted it for her it's emerald green its beautiful. tell her I think it's lovely she called her Maggie after my ma, oh god I'm greetin agane, I canny stop it Danny, it's took me nearly two hours to write this I keep gettin up and walkin away till I stop greetin, do you think dorothys alright, gonny ask my ma to phone me as soon as you get this letter , i don't have much money left, but don't ask Dorothy to phone danny, I canny talk to her, I want to but I canny.

Write to me as soon as you can danny and tell me what everybodys saying and how they all are don't leave it for three weeks danny, write to me as soon as you get this and tell Dunky and Charlie to write to me as well, Shivanw coming roon for me the night again, I think she might have more vodka, don't tell my ma.

Auntie phylis is a lot better now she seems to be back to her old self, well no really but at least shes not dead yet anyway, the district nurse has brought her a concorde, its like a chair that you lift a lid and thers a po in it for doing the toilet in, it's to save her from having to go outside, the old basterd sits on it all day just farting, she keeps standing up and asking me to check whats in it, and theres never anything but pee in it, I think she does it deliberate the smelly old cow. Micheal says he's gonny send you a book about the Irish famine, he says ther,s a lot of stuff in it you would like for your project, but he says the Scottish were nearly as bad as the English, I told him it was a hunner and thirty years ago all our family would still have been here at the time so theres no point in trying to blame us we were Irish then the same as him, and anyway he doesn't look like he's been in a famine the wee fat basterd.

I need to go shivawns coming, i'll post this tonight maybe it will get there before the one I sent last night. Write back strait away.

Lots of love

Your big sister Darlene

4/5/73

Hello Dorothy

I'll never forget you phoning me last night, I mean it for the rest of my life I'll never forget it your so brave, I know you said you understaun me no coming hame but I coodny be as brave as yo dot I just coodny, and I coodny say all the things I wanted to say last night thats why Im writing them down the day, I think your the bravest person ive ever met, if I was in your shoes i coodny have phoned you, or me ,well you know what I mean, not that I would wear any of your shoes right enough but you know what I mean. I think what you said about Daisy was beutiful and I'll never forget it, im so sorry dot I wasn't there and I'm so sorry I coodny even talk to you on the phone, im really really sorry,

and I canny believe you still wanted to ask me about what im doing, I coodny say last night cause I was greetin too much and I just wanted to hear how you were. I got off with padraig the other night, and he says he will be staying away from shivawn from now on, I've asked him to keep that wee creepy brother of his away from me, he keeps staunin too close to me and I canny stand him, he's not right in the head, i'm sure he stole a pair of my knickers off the line at the weekend, thers a pair missin and theres no way phylis would get her fat arse in them.

This is just a short letter Dorothy I'll send you anither one next week, I still don't know what to say to you really and I don't want to keep going on about all my shite, talking about shite auntie phylis has started shitting the bed again, quiet bad, I canny see her lasting much longer nobody, I'm not wishing her bad but at least if she died I could come hame, I like it hear most of the time but I do feel like coming hame sometimes as well.

Love you lots and lots

Your wee sister

Darlene.

23/7/73

Hello Danny

I'm sorry I,ve not wrote very much in the last couple of months, I have got a wee job with Padraigs family, working in the feilds its only eight pound a week but it keeps me in fags and vodka (don't tell my ma), Tell Dunky to get rid of hatchet face, I canny believe he went back with her, thanks for letting me know about Dot, I'm really glad to see she's getting back to her old self, and your right because its school holidays Charlie isnae suspended haha, and no, I don't think he should come over here for a wee holiday, I don't expect to be here for much longer, Auntie Phyliss doesn't get out of bed anymore, she canny really stand up herself without help, so thats keeping me really busy as well, theirs a lot of cleaning up after her to be done and its only me here to do it. Micheal says he sent you that book and says if you want to know any more about Cavan or the struggle whatever that is you should write to him.

I know this letters short but theres not much more I can tell you about this place unless you want to know about irritation, thats what they call putting water on the feilds, I don't know why, you and Charlie would like working in the feilds its really good apart from the feild mice I hate them.

Anyway Auntie phyliss is shouting on me I better go

Lots of love

Darlene.

15/8/73

Hello Dorothy

Dot I,ve made a really really big mistake and I don't know what too do for the best, I slept with micheal and we never used a Johnny. I canny believe I done it with him I canny stand him. Me and shivawn were going to a dance in the town hall something to day with Harvey festival or something I don't even know who he is, anyway we were sitting drinking together and she blurts out that shes pregnant to Padraig, I coodny talk, I know imagine me being speechless, I was raging I thought he was going with me, and I told her that, and she says that Padraig told her him and me worny serious that he was just keeping an eye on me for his auntie colleen until i had to go back to glesga , there getting married now, anyway.

So after she tells me this I told her to fuck off I wisnae going out with her to that dance in fact I wisnae gonny talk to her again, she new I was gone out with Paddy, how dare she, the wee fat cow. So I ran away and went into the barn behind my auntie phylises house and I took the vodka with me, I just sat there masel greetin and drinking, and then micheal came in and sat with me, I don't like the wee fat basterd but he was nice to me he put his arm round me and said how daft Paddy was that he thought I was georgious and Paddy was stupid letting me go for that wee cow shivawn.

The next thing I know he's kissing me and we ended up doing it in the barn, this was last week, I've spent all week in the house avoidin him paddy and shivawn, what if im pregnant, i canny believe I let him do that to me, and I was that drunk that I canny even remember much aboot it, he was lying on me then a bit of grunting then he got aff, he's probably telling everybody, and there all dead strict over here, they take weans aff unmarried mothers and send them to orphanages they call them illiterate or something. I wish auntie phyliss would die now so i can come hame, I know thats a teribbal thing to say but shes went completly doolaly now, she doesn't know who she is and shes got these big nappies on that the district nurse gave me, im sitting spoon feeding her like a big wean, Padraigs da said I should stop feeding her, but I canny do that, thats awful, he said thats what he would do if he had an old cow thats no use to anybody, I canny even tell if hes serius. He even said I shood haud a pilla over her face when she's sleeping, she would be glad of it and so would everybody else, I shouted at him you day it then, do you know something I think he would, I'm gonny watch the old basterd.

Gonny phone me, i want to talk to you anyway about how you are I know you said you were feeling a bit better but I still want to talk to you, I will go down to the pub next Tuesday night at eight o clock, phone me then please.

Lots of love Darlene.

That telephone conversation never took place, Auntie Phyllis died two days later and straight after the funeral Darlene made the return journey to Glasgow on her own, she returned with one big suitcase only, Colleen had promised over the phone to make sure that the rest of her cases and any other stuff which was hers would be sent over as soon as she got home from America and sorted out aunt Phyllis' house.

Darlene went and stayed with Dorothy for the first two weeks after she came back from Ireland, it turned out she wasn't pregnant after all. When she did eventually come home it was early September and she had a new job in a pickle factory, she didn't particularly like smelling of vinegar and we all got sick of beetroot and pickles very quickly. Just before Christmas Dorothy and Annie both announced they were pregnant again.

Darlene's Irish adventure perhaps didn't go exactly the way she wanted it to, but I think she enjoyed it anyway and if nothing else she missed the most traumatic event that had ever happened to our family, Daisy's death was never really talked about again, not in my hearing anyway, it probably was, between the women, because men don't really know how to handle something like that, it's not a problem that they can fix, it's too difficult and so its better not to talk about it, but it was always there, over the next few years there would be many children born into our family and they were all watched a little more than usual not that it would have made any difference, if God wanted them he would have taken them just like he did with Daisy.

Chapter seven (skint)

Put the kettle on Danny.

My da and Donnie were told four weeks before Christmas that they were being paid off it was because the company they worked for had been put on a three day week, this had something to do with the government, something about not having enough coal and electricity to last more than three days a week, whatever it was about, the result was that Donnie and my Da were sacked and we were skint.

"No Charlie, you canny get a bike for Christmas don't be bloody ridiculous son, look at us were sitting here in the dark with the light cut off, and you want a chopper, go away and don't be so bloody stupid." my Da said, he was sitting in the kitchen watching my ma try to heat a pot of water on the coal fire to make tea, our electricity had been cut off the day before, my Ma had avoided paying the previous bill thinking that she would catch up when my Da got his Christmas wage which usually included an extra weeks holiday money, so when the red bill came she had no money to pay it, so the electricity company came and cut us off, we could have the power back on when we paid the bill and the ten pound reconnection fee.

My ma could pay neither, so there was a week until Christmas and we had no electricity, luckily the heating in our house was all coal fires, unluckily the price of coal was sky high because of the miners strikes, so mostly we were burning old wood, whatever we could find really, it was a pity we had wasted all that wood on a bonfire the month before it would have come in handy now, but we went fire and wide looking for any old wood so we could have hot water, because the hot water came from the back boiler behind the coal fire. Charlie suggested cutting some of the trees down in Kinning Park, we didn't. Donnie came round with a temporary solution.

"You canny do that we'll get done" my ma said, without much conviction.

"Well its do this or sit through Christmas with no electricity" Donnie said looking at my Da. Apparently the way the electricity board would cut off your power was to remove the main fuse from the fuse box in the close which allowed electricity into your house. During a conversation with Johnnie Boyd, Donnie had learned that it was a simple matter to reconnect the electricity all you had to do was steal someone else's fuse and replace yours.

"The last time you got involved with John Boyd you ended up in jail" my Ma said shaking her head "Annie has got two weans and another one on the way, and you're going to end up in jail a few days before Christmas, for Christ sake"

"How can you get caught, if you do it through the night, how can the electric people know who done it, straight after the new year we will take it out again and nobody's any the wiser, its either that ma or yous all come to me or Dots house yous canny sit all through Christmas and the new year with no electric, what will you have for your Christmas dinner, pieces and chop pork." Donnie said grinning.

Charlie said "We canny have pieces and chopped pork for Christmas dinner it should be pieces and turkey at least."

And I added "Aye and then we can set fire to the Christmas pudding and sit round it for a heat"

Even my Ma smiled and she looked at my Da, this needed to be his decision. "Aye well I suppose it's worth a try" he said looking at Donnie "But I'll do it myself, you've got a family to look after Donald, I'll go out tonight and have a look, but are they all the same everywhere should I go a bit away from here"
My Ma said "Aye go as far as you can, because when the electricity board get told there's a fuse missing they will come straight here they know they cut us off last week"

"I don't think so Ma, they're cutting everybody off the now, it's not just me and my Da that have been laid off there's thousands of people been put on the buroo, I was down their yesterday and it was like the Barra's on Christmas eve, the place was stowed out, and I'll tell you something if it's the same tomorrow there will probably be a riot down there, the people behind the desks were right arrogant buggers, somebody gonny crack one of them on the jaw, if they're no careful, and it might be me." Donnie said.

So at two in the morning I heard My Da get up, I hadn't bothered going to sleep, it was my intention to with him. He was standing in the kitchen at the sink getting washed by candlelight, "Can I come with you Da" I whispered.

"No you Canny, go to bed Danny its two o'clock in the morning, you've got school to go to, what the hell are you doing up anyway." He whispered back.

"I'm up so I can go with you and help you" I said

"I don't need any bloody help, go to bed, I mean it, if your Ma hears you up shell kill you now get to bed" my Da said.

"I canny avoid hearing the two of you, yous are making enough noise to wake my granny up and she's been dead twenty years" my Ma said chuckling and added "put a bit of wood on that fire Danny son and see if you can get a pot of water boiled for a cup of tea, just take him with you Davie he can keep a look out for you if nothing else"

"So can I" it was Charlie wandering into the kitchen rubbing his eyes and yawning.

"No you bloody can't, my Ma said and tried to pick him up "Oh Jesus I canny even lift you, when did you get so tall, come on bedtime for you, Danny will go out and help your da, your going back to bed"

"I miss all the good stuff" he said but half heartedly, I think he was pleased enough to be going back to his nice warm bed.

"Ha ha" my Da said smiling at me "all the good stuff right enough, we're lucky we get to go out and prowl about in the rain and steal somebody's electric off them, and he's got the hardship of going back to his nice warm bed with a cuddle from his mammy, it's a poor shame for him so it is"

We walked the streets for what seemed like hours and hours but it was probably no more than one hour, I think my Da was still wrestling with his conscience, he hated thieving he really did, he considered it a complete failure of his code of honour, you just don't steal from your own.

"I don't suppose this is really stealing is it Danny" he asked rhetorically and then answered his own question "No because all that will happen is that the people who's fuse we take will phone the electric and they will replace it, after all it's not their fault is it. So really they will probably only be without electric for an hour or two. So we haven't stole anything from them, and as for the electricity board, they had no need to cut us off, I would have squared them up as soon as I got a new job, it was only a matter of time, no fuck them they should never have cut us off we've got two weans in the house they've no right to do that" he finished straightening up and walking with a little more purpose and determination

That wasn't technically true, wee Paul was still in the house but wee David was staying at Dot's until we got the light back on, he was too wee to sleep in all that cold and the bedrooms were actually getting a bit damp as well.

"Right where will we try then" he asked rubbing his hands together, either for warmth or in preparation for getting down to work.

"What about the Watsons close" I said grinning.

"He laughed and said "Oh aye the ones yous are always fighting with, why not, two birds with one stone eh?"

It was just as well I went with him, the boxes were unreachable he had to stand with his back to the wall underneath the fuse box and boost me up with his hands, we were in the Watsons close and I was trying to get the fuse box open, it had a small plastic catch on it, my Da had given me a screwdriver which let me prise open the door"

"Da" I whispered "There's no fuse in this for the Watsons house" The fuses were laid out and marked first floor left second floor right etc, and where the Watsons should be was an empty space. My Da let me down to the floor and we were both giggling and holding our hands over our mouths he whispered "So they have been cut off as well then, so much for giving them a nasty surprise in the morning" It was difficult to hold our laughter in.

"Who's will I take then" I whispered down to my Da, giggling.

"Who's down there, I can hear you, is that you Dunky McCallister, is Ina with you, you better leave her alone I know what you're after, get away from her, my Ina's a nice lassie, you just get lost." The voice hesitated and then continued "Who is it, tell me, I will wake my boys and my man up if you don't tell me who it is, getaway with you beat it, That better not be you Charlie McCallister, I know it was you that put that jobby through my door at Halloween, you better run before I get my boys up, I'm telling you" Mrs Watson half shouted half whispered from the top landing, we had obviously woke her up and she was trying to avoid waking her neighbours by the sound of it.

My Da dragged me out of the close by my collar and we ran along the paisley road for a few minutes, when we stopped it was to laugh for five minutes, I don't know what was funnier, the stupidity of what we were doing or hearing Mrs Watson chastising Dunky for corrupting her darling daughter Ina, and when my Da asked me I couldn't tell a lie, it was Charlie that put the jobby through her door at Halloween, it was a dogs jobby ,he wrapped it in a lucky bag wrapper and taped it up so it looked like it hadn't been opened he even left a couple of the wee plastic toys stuck in the jobby.

When we eventually stopped laughing I asked "What will we do then, we canny go back there"

"We will just take one out of the next close we come to, we canny do this to anybody we know" he said with resignation, he knew we had to do it but he didn't have to like it.

We took one from a close on Paisley Road West, nobody made any noise so I think it's safe to assume that they were all sleeping, I hope they didn't have an electric alarm clock or they were going to be late for work. We put it where it should go in our close, although my Da pondered this for a few minutes, he didn't want to boost me up so as I could put it in, in case I got a shock or something, and there was no way I could boost him up, eventually he recognised there was no alternative but to hold me up so I could insert it where it went, he never found it funny at all when I shouted "Bang" as I forced the fuse home, I did but and so did Charlie when I told him the next day.

My Ma refused to let us put a light on at night, she also panicked about using the electric for heating and cooking and having baths or most importantly for boiling the kettle, those were all bad enough but but she reckoned if we put the light on that the man who lived in Middleton street and worked for the electric would see it and report us. She stuck to this rule no matter how often my Da or anybody else told her that the man in Middleton street was an electrician and that didn't mean he worked for the electricity company and even if he did, there's no way he would be given a list of customers who had been cut off so he could spy on them, it was absurd. My Ma reckoned she had seen him looking up at our windows more than once, Darlene said that was probably because he fancied her, a lot of men looked up at our window trying to catch a glimpse of her, apparently.

Crime doesn't pay?

"We could rob a bank, you could come up with a plan you're supposed to have brains, and me Bobby and Searcher could do it" Charlie said.

We were lying in our beds (with the lights out obviously) it was a week before Christmas and we were trying to find a way to help the family have a better Christmas, we had already discussed the possibility of having a jumble sale at the end of the street, or trying to nick all the lead off of the roof of the factory next door, we had also considered working for it by going in to the same factory asking for old pallets and chopping them up into kindling and selling them door to door for ten pence a bundle. Charlie had suggested putting Darlene on the game, but when I pointed out she wasn't sixteen yet and that if she talked all the way through her punters would probably demand a refund he laughed and agreed it wasn't the best Idea, maybe next year if she ever lost her voice.

"We could rob a bank" he said again as if I hadn't heard him the first time.

"You talk such a lot of shite Charlie, it's easy to tell that you are related to Darlene, the both of you talk utter mince" Was my reasoned response "anyway can you imagine you and Bobby robbing a bank, if you couldn'y find a stocking to put over your heads yous would both put your heads in a pair of tights and be staggering about bumping into each other and Searcher would be behind you saying, remember I get Bobby's share as well as mine, I'm looking after it for him, no, forget about robbing a bank that's too stupid for words"

There was a moments silence as we each pondered ways of making money fast, I pondered on legal ways Charlie didn't.

"What about robbing the Fisher's guy then" Charlie suggested with no humour whatsoever in his voice.

That could be done I thought, Fishers was a department store in the middle of Glasgow city centre that allowed you to buy things on credit, furniture, clothes, toys, appliance, basically anything you would need or want in your house or indeed for Christmas. They collected your payments by coming to your house on a weekly basis and collecting your payment in cash, the man who collected my Ma's payment came on a Friday night because he knew My Da got paid on a Thursday night, he was usually there at about six o'clock having stopped at almost every close in our street and most of the surrounding streets, it was difficult to estimate how much he collected but it must have been hundreds of pounds maybe thousands.

"Think of all that money he collects Danny, and he's a wee old man, anybody could just push him over and dip his pockets, think about how that money could help my Ma and Da have a good Christmas, they would be able to get everybody the presents they wanted and probably put the electric back on so we could put a light on at night, wee Paul and Davie are gauny have a rotten Christmas if there's no presents for them, I bet it would be easy Danny, you could work out a plan for that surely" Charlie whispered excitedly into the cold air of our bedroom.

I was thinking, I was thinking that Charlie was right it would almost be a victimless crime, we wouldn't hurt the old man, we wouldn't even have to push him over, if Bobby confronted him in a close and threatened to push him over or even maybe threatened him with a knife or just pretended that he had a knife, I was thinking that the old Fisher's man would just hand over whatever cash he had and be happy not to be pushed over or stabbed, and what difference would a couple of hundred quid make to a company like Fishers, none at all. I was thinking that maybe this was possible, I was thinking I should give this a bit more thought, particularly how we could explain a sudden pile of cash to my Da.

Then I thought a bit more lucidly about my Da, where we lived was like a village and if somebody robbed the Fisher's man, absolutely everybody would know about it within hours, and if we coincidentally went to my Da with a bundle of cash and some ludicrous story about having found it, he would most likely beat us to within an inch of our lives, we weren't thieves (Electricity aside) and we absolutely were not robbers, my Da would probably take his belt to us for even thinking about terrifying and robbing an old man, and then I felt guilty for even thinking about stealing money from a harmless old guy who's worst crime was to shake his head and laugh when we all pretended not to be in on a Friday night.

"Don't be stupid Charlie, how could you have a good Christmas with stolen money, it would make it a horrible Christmas, how could we watch Paul playing with toys knowing that we scared an old man and robbed him to pay for them, it would be really horrible" I said, but Charlie never heard me he was asleep already, Charlie didn't do sleepless with guilt, that was my job.

A couple of days later on the Saturday morning and I was standing in the kitchen making tea (shockerooni) for my Ma and Dot who had stayed over the night before, she had been staying over quite a few nights recently,(without Tony). Dunky for once was also up and sitting at the table with them.

"Does anybody want some toast with their tea" I asked.

"Does the pope shit in the woods" Dunky said laughing "sorry ma" he added when he noticed the scowl on her face.

Dot smiled and said "Right then what's the plan, where are we getting money to pay for Christmas"

"You're all right, Tony's still working so you will be ok, it's only you and wee Tony anyway" Dunky said absently and then realised what he had said, "Dot I didn't mean that the way it sounded when I said you only had wee Tony I wisnae talking about Daisy, oh shit Dot I'm sorry, I'm sorry ma for saying shit as well, I should keep my stupid mouth shut so I should" He looked around presumably trying to find someone who would help him stop digging.

"I know what you meant Dunky and aye you should shut up, anyway it's not wee Tony I'm worried about it's the weans in this house and it's getting enough food in for Christmas and not to mention drink for the new year, we need to find some way of getting some money in pronto." Dot said glossing over Dunky's faux pas.

“What about the pawn” I suggested “have we got anything worth pawning”

Dot looked at the rings on her left hand as my Ma looked at hers, “I suppose we could put a few things together which might raise a few quid” Dot said “I’ve got my rings and a couple of gold chains”
“Well, I’ve got my rings and some gold chains and earrings as well” my Ma chipped in.

“What about the telly, could we no pawn that” I asked

My ma and Dot laughed and Dunky said “I don’t think radio rentals would be happy if we pawned a telly that we were renting from them”

“Anyway they’re coming out on Monday with a new telly, because we haven’t paid the rental on that one for three weeks, they’re bringing one with a coin box on the back, you will have to put fifty pence’s in it to make it work.” my Ma said quietly.

Charlie walked into the kitchen having just got out of bed “Here” he said throwing a bundle of ten pound notes on the table in front of my Ma “will that help, it’s the money I’ve been saving up all year from penny for the guy and watching cars and all that”

Dot had counted out the money there was a hundred and ten pound, a lot of pennies for the guy. I looked straight at Charlie and he looked straight back, as if he was daring me to ask where it had came from, or daring me to dispute where it had come from, because I knew and he was aware that I knew, every single penny for the guy we had managed to beg from strangers had been spent as soon as we had got it, on a new ball, on cheeseburgers and cokes in the Yellow Bird Cafe, on sweets, crisps, irn bru and strike cola and on whatever else we wasted it on at the time, where it definitely wasn’t was in Dots hands.

My Ma looked at us both and then at the money in Dots hand and said “That’s a lot of money to get from penny for the guy, Charlie, isn’t that a lot of money Danny” she looked at me, I could see she was willing me to step up and do the right thing, tell her where it had come from, if I knew or at least tell her it wasn't as Charlie said.

I looked her right in the eye and said "I knew he was nicking most of the money we were making, sometimes I thought we might be making a tenner but when we got up to the house and counted it there was only five or six quid there, he must have been robbing me and hiding it all away, half of that money's mine then Charlie" I tried to look convincing in my indignation, but nobody bought it, but nobody disputed it either, it was a hundred and ten quid, it wouldn't guarantee a happy Christmas but it might help, and if it was dubious where it had came from then so what, we were sitting drinking tea made with water boiled by stolen electricity.

At Hogmanay my Da would probably drink whisky from a bottle which he bought from a guy in the pub who worked in a distillery and always managed to get his pals some cheap whisky at Christmas, some of the toys the children would find with delight under the tree would have come from the Barra's market and when my Ma paid for them the stallholder would be laughing at how much of a miracle it was that they didn't break when they fell off the back of the lorry.

So that was that, nobody thought of asking Charlie how he had managed to turn all of that loose change into ten pound notes, and when Dot suggested that nobody should mention this to my Dam because he was feeling bad enough about us struggling to have a Christmas, nobody disagreed.

Later that evening Darlene ran into the kitchen with her usual exuberance "Somebody mugged old Mr Anderson" she shouted excitedly.

"Who's old Mr Anderson" my Da asked.

"The old man from Fisher's that comes here on a Friday, he's a nice old man, he gave me a packet of polo mints once, it was because I was polite when I answered the door, and told him my Ma was out at the shops, even though my Ma was hiding behind her bedroom door, he said thanks hen, people usually just let me stand outside for ages hoping I'll go away, at least you opened the door and told me I'm no getting paid" Darlene said breathlessly.

"Ok Darlene slow down, who said he got mugged and when was it" my Ma said, glancing at me, I kept my head down and refused to acknowledge her glance.

"Last night it was, round in Midlock Street, it must have been about seven o'clock because I seen him leaving our street after half past six" Darlene started her story eagerly.

"Was he here at our house last night" my Da asked, as my Ma shook her head with a No on her lips Darlene said "Da I'm trying to tell you what happened, it was terrible"

My Ma then interrupted "Was Mr Anderson hurt "

"Aw Ma gaunny let me tell you what happened, the whole story" Darlene said upset at being cut off in full flow.

"Tell us then for god's sake Darlene but don't drag it out into a bedtime story will you" my Da said smiling.

"Right, me and Theresa Green seen him leaving the end of our street at about half past six, he had just come out of Mrs Wilsons close, the old woman with the wee black dug that nearly got knocked down in the summer, do you remember I told you about that it was a co-op van.."

"Darlene" was all my Ma had to say to get her back on track.

"So anyway do you know Mr Jackson that lives on Midlock street, you always see him walking about with a black coat and an old fashioned hat on, even in the summer" She glanced at my Da who was clearly losing his patience and looked as if he was just going to walk away, so she started talking even faster.

“well anyway he had just left Mr Jacksons close when he got mugged and wait for this you’ll never believe it” my Ma again glanced at me, and again I refused to acknowledge her glance, I couldn’t anyway even if I had wanted to, I was petrified of what Darlene was about to say.

“He thinks it was a father and son that mugged him, he said two people pushed him back into the close and said to him, give us the money auld yin and you don’t have to get hurt, it’s no your money anyway so don’t even think about fighting for it, this was the big guy that said it the one he thought might be the father, and then the wee boy said don’t fight mister it’s no worth it, or something like that anyway he gave them the money, nearly four hundred pound he said, imagine that four hundred pound, I could get all the clothes in Shapiro’s for four hundred quid”

My Da said “Lucky he didnae fight, there’s some right bastards about, wouldn’t think twice about hitting an old guy, shitebags they wouldn’t try that with me or anybody else capable of standing up to them how can they do that at Christmas, how could they go away and spend that money on Christmas presents for their family, right enough they probably won’t it’ll go on drink probably, bastards I hope the police get them”

This almost constituted a speech from my Da, for at least the third time My Ma glanced at me and for at least the third time I refused to look back. I understood the father and son reference, in the dark bobby did look like a big guy and Searcher was only about five foot one, but where was Charlie in this, then I got it, he was keeping the edge, the lookout, he was standing outside the close ready to shout at the slightest sign of trouble, or he was in the close with Bobby and Searcher kept the edge. I turned and walked out of the kitchen without looking at my Ma or Da, I was too transparent.

I heard Darlene say as a I closed my bedroom door “I know it’s really bad but imagine having four hundred quid right now, we would have a great Christmas” and my Da said “Darlene hen, you canny have a good

Christmas on somebody else's shoulders sweetheart, not if you have got any conscience you canny"

Have yourself a merry little Christmas

The next two days passed slowly, Charlie and I struggled to settle our differences both of us would be looking at Christmas morning through a black eye or two (one for him two for me), it was Christmas eve, Dot and my Ma had pawned their rings, Dunky had chipped in a week's wages, Tony had sent Dot up forty pounds in an envelope, she threw that into the pot as well, my Da gave my Ma fifty quid, I don't know where he got that he never said. Anyway between them my Ma and Dot had got everything in for our normal family Christmas, albeit none of us would be getting anything extravagant but everybody had a few presents under the tree and all the necessary food and drink was making the shelves creak in the kitchen like any other year.

I was lying on my bed reading a book and basically trying to avoid Charlie, I had had enough of fighting he was never going to agree with me and after all, despite what my parents thought it wasn't my job to keep him on the straight and narrow, I had tried, I was always trying, he heard my Ma and Da saying all the same things that I heard them say, so why did I know he was out of order but he didn't, I wasn't even fourteen yet but I knew what he was getting into was no longer cheeky wee boys being cheeky wee boys, it was getting serious and I know he was only twelve but he was Glasgow streetwise twelve which equals eighteen or twenty anywhere else.

"What's up Danny, is everybody boring you again is that why your face is in a book as usual" Charlie sarcastically uttered as he stepped into the bedroom we shared.

"Piss off Charlie, I mean it, if you don't want a broken jaw to go with your black eye just fuck off, I'm telling you" I said with intense anger and Charlie knew it, I could see in his face that he was struggling with a decision should he walk out with a smart mouth comment thrown over his shoulder or leap on top of me for round six or seven or two hundred and twenty or whatever round it was in our never ending boxing match.

I pretended not to notice his dilemma and turned to the next page in my book, which by now I wasn't reading, I was too busy watching him out of the corner of my eye and bracing myself for the inevitable lunge and flurry of punches which were bound to figure in my immediate future.

"Enough both of you" my Ma said as she pushed Charlie gently into the room, as he turned she handed him a bundle of money.

"Here son, we didn't need that money after all, you can put it away again and use it for whatever it was you were saving up for, it must have been important if you were prepared to steal for it" Charlie eyes widened. "Off your brother I mean" my Ma added with a searching look at Charlie, we all know that's not what she meant.

"By rights Danny, he should give half of that money to you really" my Ma said looking straight at Charlie. "After all you both earned it doing penny for the guy"

Charlie looked at her and then at me and he said "Take half of it if you want Danny"

"No" I said with obvious disdain "You earned it Charlie, I was only standing there you did all the hard work, keep it, it's all yours, you deserve it." I then turned to the wall and continued reading my book, I never seen my ma's face as she walked out of the room but I heard her sigh and if that sigh couldn't put Charlie off then nothing ever would. I wish I could tell you Charlie did something good with that money like gave it to the Salvation Army or bought his wee brothers some fantastic toys, he didn't, Charlie bought himself a chopper in the January sales.

Paul was absolutely delighted on Christmas morning he got a wee three wheeler trike and a red Indian headdress and tomahawk to play with and since he had started talking recently he was loving telling everybody what he had got from Santa, the only down side to him starting to talk was when he burst into my Da's bedroom brandishing the tomahawk above his head and shouting "Look what I got Da, I'm gauny cut your balls off" we all found it immensely funny, my Ma didn't she insisted all day that he had been saying cut your paws off, but she eventually agreed that didn't make sense and had a good laugh thinking about my Da's face when he looked up after what Paul had said.

We were having a normal lovely family Christmas without much drama this time, no police visits no waters breaking, no dramatics at all really, there's no way that was going to last the whole day. Donald and Annie came round as usual for their dinner, with the two weans in tow and she was already starting to show a bit with her third, Annie came into the kitchen with my Ma and Dot to help with peeling the vegetables, I got the sprouts to do as usual, cut off the stub carve in an x, cut off the stub carve in an x, about a thousand times.

Annie pushed the door closed and said "Has your Da been borrowing money from Mr Logan Dot?" It was my Ma that answered.

"Absolutely not Annie, where did you hear that? She asked incredulously.

"My Da said he heard somebody saying in the pub that your Davie was tapping money from Mr Logan and that Mr Logan was bragging about having Davie McCallister by the baws" Annie replied reluctantly, looking at my Ma as if she was waiting for an explosion.

"Well you tell your Da when you see him that Davie McCallister never borrowed anything off that one armed bandit and never would" my Ma said banging the turkey on to the kitchen work top ready for stuffing, the turkey had been dead for quite a while I think but I bet it still felt pain the way she banged it down.

“I’m just telling you what I heard Maggie, I didn’t think it would be true, I know how Davie hates that wee nyaff Logan” Annie said and then wisely said no more.

I had never heard of this Mr Logan, I found out later that he was a money lender who held court in the Old Toll Bar he sat in a corner smoking cigars and drinking Grouse whiskey and generally lording it over everybody less fortunate than himself, he was fat and greasy and obnoxious. There were usually at least two of his minders loitering about at the bar, they were the guys that would come and collect the debt if you didn’t turn up on a Saturday morning with your weekly payment. He wasn’t the worst of the loan sharks, the worst ones were to be found in pubs even seedier than The Old Toll Bar, like the Iron Man in Govan, those guys charged a hundred per cent interest per week, if you borrowed a tenner on a Monday you had to pay twenty quid by the following Monday if you didn’t it would be forty quid the next week or eighty quid the week after until such times as they decided you weren’t willing to pay and they broke some (or all) of your bones.

Mr Logan wasn’t like that he was more sly, he gave you the money and you told him when you could pay it back and then he would tell you how much you had to pay back, for instance let’s say you weren’t working and you asked him for a loan of fifty quid at Christmas and told him you would pay him back at the end of January, if he trusted you and knew you reasonably well he might say “No bother you give me back eighty quid and we will shake hands” and then write it in his little book. Now if he didn’t particularly like you he would say “Ok but it’s gauny mean you need to pay me back a hundred and twenty and if you don’t one of the ugly boys will be round to see you” and worst of all if you were a single woman maybe a widow with a family or a young lassie with a man in jail then he would laugh lasciviously and say “There’s more than one way to pay off a debt” he had even been accused of saying this to married women in the past, and collecting it apparently.

My Da hated him, more than once my Da had passed remarks in that particular pub about the smell that lingered in the corner, in a voice which was meant to be overheard, it all went back apparently to one incident where this Mr Logan had said something to my Ma about her not having any worries paying him back with cash if she ever needed to borrow money, he was sure they could come to an easier arrangement. It was only his two big minders that had stopped my Da from getting at him that time, there had been several near things after that as well, the opinion of the pub goers of the paisley road west was generally that if Mr Logan ever turned up in the same pub without his minders as Davie McCallister then he would be paying a visit to casualty that night, or if Davie McCallister got sufficiently drunk one night it would be him in casualty after trying to take on the two minders.

It was a bit later that I found out that Mr Logan had come into the money he now used to prop up his loan business because of an accident, one of his arms had been torn off by a faulty machine when he worked in a cement factory and he had got a couple of thousand pounds in compensation. The rumour was that he had done it deliberately because the same thing had happened the year before to someone else. That explained my Ma's remark when she called him the one armed bandit, I had actually thought at first she meant my Da hadn't borrowed money from a fruit machine.

That put a bit of a dampener on Christmas dinner it was obvious that this was probably the fifty quid my Da had given my Ma a couple of days before, and maybe she would have asked him about it as it happens she didn't, Donnie did.

"What's this crap Peter Logan's spouting Da about giving you a loan of fifty quid and telling everybody he's got you by the baws, is he just asking for trouble or what" Donald asked between the soup and the turkey and right in the middle of his sixth can of Tennent's lager.

My Da who was also on at least his sixth can of McEwans export said "Crap is right enough Donnie, I wouldn't ask that arse for a drink of water if I was dying of thirst, where did you hear this shit anyway?"

"Annie's old man told me the one armed bandit was pished on Friday night and telling everybody in the old toll how he was gauny put you in your place" Donnie replied, the rest of us fell silent, my Da was moody at the best of times but this was not going to be good, not at all, this was going to be a long way from good.

"Well, I better go down there the day after boxing day and ask him nicely to let go of my baws then, if he hasn't squeezed them to death by then I mean" he said and laughed out loud with Donnie, of all the reactions I expected laughter wasn't one of them. My Ma didn't laugh she was looking carefully at my Da because she could see then what I would only see years later, when my Da laughed look at his eyes because if they weren't laughing along with his mouth get out of the way. Quick.

I was laughing along with him and Donnie when my Da looked at me and said "Is that funny Danny boy, a one armed arsehole trying to take the pish out of your Da, do you think that's really funny son" with more menace in his voice than I wanted to hear. Charlie decided me getting shouted at was funny so he decided to snigger at probably the worst probable moment.

"Oh so now it's the bold Charlie that thinks he can laugh at his Da, is that what I am, a fuckin laughing stock to this family." my Da said pushing his plate away with enough force to knock over a glass of Irn Bru Darlene had in front of her.

Darlene screeched "Nobody's laughing at you, why do you have to ruin everything" and then stomped out of the room crying."

My Da pulled his plate back in front of him and said "What's the matter with her, is she due her monthlies or something, what a performance, go and tell her to come eat her turkey before it gets cold, Charlie son"

Charlie looked at me, I'm not sure why, probably expecting me to go and try to persuade Darlene back to the table, because sometimes she listened to me or maybe he was just being his usual self, a lazy wee shit that didn't want to move.

"What the fuck are you looking at him for" my Da raged "do you need his permission to do what I tell you, no you don't, you just do what I tell you when I tell you" He turned to my Ma "what the fuck is going on here, why is nobody in this house doing what I tell them, this is all your fuckin fault, what have you been telling them, that because I'm no working and no putting food on the table they can treat me any way they want, well they canny" and he threw his plate of Christmas dinner over my Ma's head and with more luck than judgement it hit the curtain rather than the window and fell to the floor with a quiet thud.

Wee Davie started wailing and Paul started greetin as well, he didn't understand how it had went from laughing and joking to shouting and bawling within seconds, he would soon learn to understand, the rest of us had.

My Da pushed away from the table and stormed out of the room pushing a standard lamp over as he passed it causing the bulb to explode with a soft whimper. I looked at my Ma, there were tears on both of her cheeks, she just stared in front of her avoiding eye contact with her own children, she did eventually glance at Dorothy, whose anger was clearly visible, and Dorothy did tend to wear her heart on her sleeve.

Charlie looked at me, grinned and continued eating his Christmas dinner, Dunky muttered "For fuck sake" under his breath and shook his head before pushing his plate forward and standing up.

"Sit down Duncan and finish your dinner, there's trifle after that as well, it wasn't easy putting this dinner on the table and it's no going in the bloody bin, and mind your language as well there's no need for cursing like that" my Ma said as she picked up her own knife and fork and began eating, there's no way she was tasting any of that food, well I know I couldn't taste mine.

Darlene flounced back into the room, "I'm finishing my dinner, I was enjoying that ma, and it's not my fault he's haemorrhoid" and when we all laughed she said "paranoid I mean" and giggled as she sat back down, this at least broke the tension enough for us to finish eating our food, but it didn't do anything to fill in the massive hole my Da's empty chair made.

The rest of the afternoon and early evening passed very quietly, all the youngest children took very little notice of the tension, they just got on with ripping into their selection boxes and gorging themselves on chocolate, Darlene had a short argument with my Ma because she wanted to go out with her pals and my Ma said "It's Christmas, you could stay in for one night and play with your wee brothers and your nephews and niece."

Darlene looked at my Ma with total bewilderment on her face and whined "Are you serious Ma, you think I should stay in and play at cowboy and Indians with Paul, I'm sixteen Ma, and why would I stay in here anyway to wait for the next instalment of a family at war, I don't think so" she stood waiting for my Ma to decide, her arms were again crossed over her chest in her usual pose of defiance, it's no wonder her boobs wouldn't grow she was probably holding them back by having her arms crossed over them all the time.

My Ma sighed "Go out I suppose, but you better no be drinking I'm sure I smelled whisky on your breath the other night"

Even though she had won the argument Darlene still strutted out in a mood tossing her hair and swinging her arms. Dunky then sarcastically said to my Ma "I've finished playing cowboys and Indians with Paul and Mark, Danny doesn't want a game of chess and Charlie doesn't want to play with me and I'm nearly eighteen can I go out and play with my pals as well, and I promise to be careful with the amount of alcohol I consume, please can I go out, pretty please"

This almost brought a smile to my Ma's face but not quite she said "Go out if you want but if you're out chasing lassies again, you better be careful"

Annie laughed and said "If you're talking about safe sex Maggie, Dunky thinks that means no telling the lassie your real name" then she realised she was talking to my Ma and went bright red.

My Da then walked back into the living room as if nothing had happened and sat down in the chair nearest the fire and said "Have you seen what that Darlene's wearing, that skirt she has on barely covers her arse it's more like a bloody belt than a skirt, and she will catch her death of cold if she doesn't put a coat on"

Darlene could just about be heard going out the front door saying "I don't tell him he canny wear the stupid jumpers do I?" and slammed the door behind her.

"She's turning into a right wee madam, you let her away with murder" my Da said settling into the armchair and telling Charlie "Turn that telly to ITV and go and get me a McEwans export out of the fridge." Charlie did as he was told without looking at anybody at all. (Miracles do happen)

I decided this was a good time to get out of the living room before my Da decided I was getting on his nerves for some reason, I went into the kitchen for a glass of water but before I could escape Annie and Dot were right behind me. Annie grabbed me from behind and picked me up kissing the back of my neck three or four times "Put the kettle on Danny and then give us a wee hand to do all these dishes, leave your ma and Da to watch a wee bit of telly, there a good boy"

"If you want me to make tea, just ask, you don't need to slabber all down the back of my neck" I said feigning annoyance.

“Ha, ha you keep complaining Danny but I think you like my wee kisses don’t you really” Annie said laughing and grabbing me again trying to plant more kisses on my cheeks.

“Beat it and leave me alone or you can make your own tea” I said struggling free.

“Cut me a slice of that Christmas cake that’s in the fridge Danny with my tea, I am eating for two you know” Annie said letting me go and sitting at the table beside Dot.

“Oh that’s good” I replied “It’s about time you cut down a bit” She missed me with the Brussel sprout she threw but only just.

“What was that all about with your Da Dorothy “ Annie asked “ he went a bit mental did he no, I know Donnie’s been fed up no working as well and he’s moping about the house all the time but something will turn up for them it always does, but your Da’s in a right bad mood isn’t he”

“Aye he is and he will probably take it out on her later on, if he keeps drinking, I don’t know why she keeps taking it, I would jail Tony if he treated me like that or stab him” she said and giggled as if she was joking. Annie and I both knew she wasn’t.

“Och you’re Da’s no that bad Dot, Aye all right he gives Maggie the occasional slap or wee shiner now and again, but at least he’s out working most of the time and handing his money in, It’s no as if he gambles it all away or drinks the lot of it is it?, there’s a lot worse than him, I mean look at that Geordie Burns in Blackburn street, do you remember him, he murdered his wife and kept her in the outside toilet for two weeks until his neighbours noticed the smell, the old woman next door to him told me that even during the two weeks she was lying dead in there, he still used the toilet, how could you, my god can you imagine, a dead woman staring at you when you’re trying to do your business, it gives me the heebie jeebies” Annie said shuddering.

"I don't suppose she would have been staring at him, her eyes were probably shut and he would have his back to her when he was peeing, right enough when he was having a jobby he would be looking right at her" I offered as my part of the conversation.

"Shut up Danny, why are wee boys so bloody disgusting" Dorothy said looking at me and shaking her head. " I know he's no that bad Annie, there are much worse than him, I know that but It's not fair my Ma's doing as much as she can to bring money in while he's not working, but even the schools have been on a three day week and they've cut back on her hours, and he won't sign on the buroo he says it's like begging, well he needs to bloody beg my Ma's skint and she will need to get that jewellery out of the pawn after the New Year, he could be doing a bit more"

Annie grinned and said "They're no that skint really Dot, I remember when you all lived in Mclean street and you were really skint, it was pieces and chips for your dinner every night, and that was only because somebody rigged the electric so you could get your chip pan on, if you couldn't get it on it was pieces and stork margarine, and you're light was hardly ever on, no that my house was any better right enough we used candles for years we didn't know what it was to have a meal that wasn't cooked on the coal fire, that's if we could afford coal, most of the time my brothers went about with that old pram collecting old bits of wood to burn"

"Aye I remember your brothers pushing that about all the time" Dot also grinned at her recollections and replied "I remember you used to babysit for Danny and Charlie and I used to go mad at my Ma, whenever you turned up at the door and asked if you could take the boys out in the pram, I used to tell her I wanted to take them out"

"Why, you hated taking them out, you were always moaning about it, I used to take them everywhere down the Clydeside up to Glasgow Green I walked all the way into paisley town centre one day right past Barrshaw park, and I bet you don't remember that Danny" Annie said ruffling my hair "I used to babysit you and Charlie, I used to change your nappies, I had to wash your bum and make sure your wee man was clean" she started cackling then and almost choked on her slice of Christmas cake, I didn't see what was so funny.

Dot laughed at my embarrassment and then continued "No, I know I didn't want to take them out but I wanted to take the pram out, me and the boys I hung about with used to use it to take scrap lead over to Partick on the ferry, you should have seen us trying to load it on to the ferry it took about five of us to pull it up one step, anybody that seen us must have thought it was a baby elephant we had in it. We nearly dropped Charlie in the Clyde one day, the pram got stuck in the wee space between the ferry and the steps you go down to get onto the ferry, and Charlie wasn't strapped in, I was pulling and hauling at the pram and he nearly fell over the side into the water, one of the boys with me grabbed him just before he tumbled out of the pram, I absolutely shit myself, can you imagine it, coming home and telling my Ma, I had dropped Charlie in the River Clyde."

"It wouldn't have bothered me" I said flippantly.

"Oh Danny don't say that, he's your wee brother and by the way, he worships you he's like your wee dog, whenever he comes in the house the first thing he does is look for you and if anybody ever says anything about you he's right into them, I don't know how many times I've had to pull him off of Dunky, don't be a wee shite and say that you don't care, it's just no true" Annie said.

Wow, how does he do it? How does he fool everybody? Is he actually a demon that convinces everybody he's a saint and I'm the only one that can see his inner self, he's a horrible wee shite and always has been, aye he could be the most generous of people at times and I suppose he did watch my back always, and we did have a laugh together most of the time, and I suppose in some ways Annie was right he could be like a wee dog, for instance it took me months to get him to stop pishing in the corner of the bedroom.

Dot said "You know talking about Dunky, how come he's never in the kitchen anymore, it used to be he was under your feet all the time trying to learn to cook, he was forever wanting to chop vegetables and asking how to make soup and how do you brown mince or stew and how long does everything take in the oven, you never see him in here anymore"

"What are you talking about we weren't even talking about Dunky, are you Darlene in disguise" I asked.

"Don't be cheeky Danny, I can still pull your trousers down and skelp your arse, you're no too big" Dot said and Annie laughed and said "Aye and I can help her, after all I've seen it all before" and started cackling again.

"You two need to grow up" I said "In the head but not in the belly, yous are both grown up enough there" and ran out of the kitchen cackling just like Annie does.

And a happy new year

It could have been a relatively happy new year I suppose, both my Da and Donnie got offered a job working in Corby, in England somewhere the money was quite good but it was back to just coming home the occasional weekend. Corby was known as Little Scotland at the time and I think it might still be known as that to this day. So that put my Da in a much better mood, they got offered the job two nights before hogmanay and one night before they got the jail for doing grievous bodily harm to Peter Logan the one armed bandit.

I wasn't there obviously it had happened in the Red Lion pub, Dunky was there and involved but he managed to get away and run home to tell my Ma, although I'm not sure what he expected her to be able to do, we were sitting watching are you being served, tomorrows world was just finished so it must have been between half seven and eight o'clock.

“Ma, ma, my Da’s got lifted by the polis” Dunky said bursting into the living room breathless.

“What for, why, when, what happened, who told you that” were questions all fired at him at once by my Ma Darlene me and Charlie.

“Wait a minute, hold on, I canny breath, I’ve just ran all the way from the Red Lion, through all the back courts, I’m knackered I must have climbed twenty walls, hold on let me get my breath” he panted as he sat on the couch next to my Ma.

He got control of his breath and said “I was going along the Paisley Road to meet Mary Simpson, I was meeting her outside Woolworths”

Darlene interrupted. “Mary Simpson, the nurse’s wee sister, she’s nice, a cut above your normal kind of lassie Dunky, where did you meet her, and why is she...”

“Shut up Darlene” said me my Ma and Charlie at the same time.

Dunky just smiled at Darlene and carried on with his tale “Anyway, I met my Da and Donnie coming off the bus and they asked me if I wanted to come into the Red Lion for a pint, I thought it might be a bit tight for time but never mind she would probably wait for me, they always do.”

“All right Casanova, just get on with it, what happened to my Da” I said, he couldn’t charm me the way he did all the women, well most of the women.

“Aye right ok, so I went in for a pint with them and who was sitting at the bar, if it wasn’t Peter Logan, on his tod, none of his heavies in sight, and my Da just laughed and said “Well, well it’s the prick with one arm” and Logan answered him, ”It’s all been a bit of a misunderstanding Davie, I gave Willie Mulgrew a loan of fifty quid and he told me it was for you, I thought he meant you sent him in to borrow it for you, I never knew he was getting it for himself to pay you what he owed you, how was I supposed to know that, anyway no hard feelings eh?”

“Well you know what my Da’s like when he’s getting ready to fight, he starts acting like it’s all a big joke ducking and diving kidding on he’s just messing about, it’s all a bit of fun until he got close enough to Logan and then he just lamped him one right on the jaw, Logan is fat, you know that ,but you should have seen it, he just went flying off the stool he was sitting on, right on to a table behind where three old men were sitting playing dominoes, ha ha ,when Logan’s head banged off the table one of the old yins said “Is that you Chapping Peter”, It was dead funny, well no for Logan I suppose he was trying to get up but he was staggering all over the place waving his one good arm about trying to swipe it at my Da”

Dunky paused for breath and took a drink from the glass of Irn Bru I had in my hand and then went on “Anyway me and Donnie are standing saying, you deserve everything you get you fat bastard and get in to him Da don’t let him get back up, it was bad I know because me and Donnie were standing laughing at Logan trying to fight my Da, even with two arms and five stone lighter he wouldn’t have had a chance, well it didn’t stay funny for long, the pub door opened and Logan’s two minders came in, they must have been away breaking somebody’s legs or something.”

“Donnie didn’t even wait for them to say anything he jumped right up on a chair and tried to stick the head on the nearest one, don’t say anything to him right, but even on the chair he couldn’t reach the guys face, but he stuck the head on his neck and the guy went down choking, I threw a chair at the other one and when he ducked out of the way my Da went for him, and then it was just pandemonium, a chair went flying right into the gantry and smashed all the optics to bits, then the next thing I know somebody picked me up and threw me over the bar, I was lucky the way I landed I was all right” Dunky paused.

“Why did you land on your head” Charlie asked. “Shush” my ma said and “where are your Da and Donnie now”

“They got lifted but wait a minute I’ll get to that, so anyway, everybody’s going mental, my Da and one of the heavies are rolling about on the floor, and my Da’s trying to bite his ear off and the big guys screaming like Darlene in a shoe shop with no money, Donnie’s under a table now with the other heavy he’s getting a bit of a doing cause the other guys massive, but he’s giving it a right good go, and then Logan picks up one of them big bottles of Bells whisky, you know the empty one on the bar they fill with coppers for the weans home at Christmas, well he picks it up above his head with his one hand, probably because it was empty, they’re right heavy when their full, ready to brain my Da with it, then one of the old boys pushes him in the back, I seen what one done it, I’ll nick in there tomorrow and see the old boy alright for a drink or three, so Logan stumbles and falls and as he falls the bells bottle smashes off the bar and Logan falls onto the bit that’s left in his hand, he stabbed himself right in the guts with it, You should have seen the blood, just at that the doors burst open and in come the polis, they take one look at Logan and huckle my Da and Donnie, well they’re no gonny ask any questions are they, I think half of them owe Logan money and the other half used to owe him money, so that was it they were both huckled, Donnie was still trying to kick that big guy in the balls as the polis were dragging him out to the van. The only polis that spoke to me was Archie Brown, he said to come and tell you my Da would probably get done with GBH and you better get a lawyer down to Orkney Street, this one could be serious.” Dunky drew in a deep breath and then let it out, unbelievable man, you should have seen Donnie trying to header that big gorilla, it was brilliant, brave as lion I mean it”

“Or as daft as a brush” my Ma said, “so how come they let you go”

“I wasn’t actually doing anything when they came in, I was standing in behind the bar I had just stood up after the big guy threw me over it, so I just started talking to the barmaid when I seen the polis coming in” Dunky grinned. “She was quite tasty as well by the way, I hope she’s working tomorrow when I go in and buy the old guy a half”

"There's always a silver lining isn't their Dunky" I said. He just grinned again and winked at me.

"Well there's nothing we can do tonight, we will need to wait till the morning and see if we can get them a lawyer, they won't go to court until the morning anyway" my Ma said.

"Right ok, I'm going to bolt along and see if Mary Simpson is still there" Dunky said standing up and straightening his hair and running his fingers down the side of his face , he was trying to grow sideburns like Noddy Holder but without much success.

"Leave your bum fluff alone Dunky, Mary Simpson won't still be there, you were supposed to meet her an hour and a half ago" my Ma said.

She probably will be", Darlene said sighing at the depth of stupidity girls show when Dunky is involved.

It was a long night, my Ma must have sat up all night because when I got up at eight o'clock she was sitting up in the armchair at the fire with a cup of tea in her hand and her head down, and she still had the same clothes on from the night before.

"Do you want more tea Ma" I asked quietly, I didn't want to startle her, she seemed lost in thought.

"Aye, Danny that would be nice son, then I will go and get dressed, I suppose I better try and get a lawyer for them two dafties eh?, I don't know how we can afford it but, I thought maybe with your Da and Donnie getting this job down in Corby that we might get back on our feet a wee bit, but now this, if your Da gets the jail we could all be out on the street" She started crying, not loudly just tears running down her cheek.

I didn't have a clue what to do, I was only thirteen , I don't think a thirteen year old telling her everything would be alright and not to worry would make much difference to her, so I sat on the floor at her feet and put my head on her knee and my arms round her legs and held on, she seemed to take some comfort from just rubbing my head, I know I did, and after a few minutes she had composed herself and she said "Right we will get nowhere sitting feeling sorry for ourselves, kettle on, and make me two slices of toast with some of your Da's butter, if he's going to Barlinnie, he's not going to need that is he?".

I was reluctant to let go, this was going to be a terribly difficult time for her and young as I was I wanted to try and protect her, I knew I couldn't but that didn't stop me from wishing I could.

"Right people, its Hogmanay, who's going for the stew for the steak pie and who's going for the carry out?" shouted my Da from the hall.

He came into the living room with Donnie behind them, and I jumped up "I thought yous were in Barlinnie, Dunky says yous near killed that Logan guy" I said bewildered by their presence. Bewildered but very pleased, my Da was here and everything was going to be ok, I turned to my Ma expecting to see signs of her happiness at their release on her face but there was none. I thought it strange that she wasn't happy to see them, but then I was young and didn't realise that they way my Ma probably seen it was that she had sat up all night worrying about what was to become of her family, because of her husband's foolish pride, she was worried about the very basic need to feed and shelter her family, my Da had probably been worried all night about missing out on Hogmanay.

My Da said "Peter Logan refused to give the polis a statement about what happened he said he couldn't remember what started the boxing, all he could remember was getting pushed in the back, probably accidentally, and falling on to a broken bottle, and the two galoots that were with him said they were trying to break up the fighting and didn't actually see who was hitting who, so the polis couldn't charge anybody, they thought about charging both of us with drunk and disorderly but when they realised that we hadn't even had a single pint they couldn't even do that. So here we are ready for Hogmanay, but a cup of tea and a piece and sausage will do us just now Danny boy!" and he slapped his hands and rubbed them together, he barely looked at my Ma, and she put her head down and carried on drinking her cold tea.

"What's the matter with your face, they let me go, problem solved" my Da said to my Ma in a tone of voice which suggested he was surprised by her lack of celebration.

"Problem solved is it, and what do you think Peter Logan is going to do next, do you think he's going to shake hands and say, it's all right Davie, I know I'm a money lender and I need people to be scared of me and my minders, but I'm not going to bother getting back at you, because you're a good guy really, and if everybody knows I let you away with putting me in hospital they'll understand because of how good a guy you are. Or do you think maybe he will get somebody to kick your head in some night when you're steaming drunk and crawling along Paisley road, or maybe somebody to stab you in the back when you're standing at the toilet in some manky pub, and when you're in hospital, do you think the magic money fairies are going to come and say here Maggie there's enough to pay the rent and the electricity, now when your gas bill comes don't forget to let us know and don't let your weans go hungry just ask us, nothings too much trouble because your Davie's one of the good guys" She was out of breath by the time she had finished and crying again but she had enough puff left to say "For Christ's sake Davie when will you grow up"

She stood up and left the room, shuffling between my Da and Donnie, who at least had the sense to say nothing. I think that was the first time I ever thought my Ma looked old. My Da turned to me and Donnie hands spread wide palms pointing upwards and said "What was that all about, she needs to cheer up a bit it's the bells tonight" and he laughed and slapped Donnie on the back. Donnie smiled at him but hesitantly, "Aye Da, it's the bells right enough, but maybe no in this house"

My ma eventually gave in to the building excitement of Hogmanay, it would really have been unthinkable for us not to throw open our doors to our friends and neighbours, it was what we did, the McCallister's parties already had a good reputation for being good for a laugh and a sing song and plenty of grub, just bring your own bottle and enjoy yourself, this was only our third Hogmanay in Cessnock, but people had started asking on boxing day whether we would be having our usual party at the bells, of course we would, and my Ma even agreed that we could turn the lights on as long as we all kept an eye out for the man from the electricity board.

So 1973 finished up pretty much as it had started with a drunken party, the main difference being that Colleen our Irish cousin wasn't there this year, which left Darlene to be the centre of attention which suited her down to the ground, she had come back from Ireland a bit depressed probably because she had to come back home and then there was the situation with Daisy, Darlene seemed to have taken that very hard, obviously because she wasn't there when it happened, but as the rest of the year passed Darlene went from a girl into a women, there were no socks down her bra this year.

She had probably grown up more than any of us during this year, but then Charlie had moved up a level in his development as well, the things he was getting into now weren't just pranks, ask the Fisher's man. I would be fourteen this year and Charlie would be twelve, I had made my decision I intended to do well at school, get some qualifications and get a decent job, make my Ma proud if I could, it seemed to matter to her that I showed some academic promise, I never felt as if I was very good at anything, I always tried hard but there was always somebody faster, taller, bigger than me, maybe school was my chance to stand out from the crowd.

Charlie was on the threshold of making his decision, which way he wanted his life to go, so far he wasn't very academic, smart yes, much smarter than me, as streetwise as anybody I ever met, but which way would he go, would he follow his heart or follow the money, time would tell, I suppose.

Chapter eight (Responsibility and irresponsibility)

Home alone

"So when will you be able to come home then" my Ma asked my Da, it was the night before Donnie and my Da had to catch the train to Corby they would be working down there for at least a year, which was fantastic for all of us, there was still a three day week in a lot of places and strikes and everything else going on, but they would be living in Corby and working virtually seven days a week, apparently a steel plant or something was being dismantled and it had to be done as quick as possible so they would have no time off at all for the first few months anyway. The money was exceptionally good and my Ma had at last cheered up a bit, nothing had happened yet after that incident with peter Logan, but none of us were daft, we knew something would, eventually, but if My Da and Donnie were going to be away for the best part of a year, the whole thing might just blow over, or more likely Logan would move on to somebody else, and with a bit of luck somebody else would do him in.

Donnie again had massive reservations about going away and leaving Annie on her own, not that he was worried about how she would cope with her two toddlers and the third one currently cooking in her oven, no he was more worried about her finding somebody else, which Annie treated with scorn and derision, if anything she would say he was much more likely to play away than she was. There had been many nights Annie had wandered the streets of Cessnock and Ibrox searching for Donnie, dragging her children about in a big pram in the middle of the night, and when she eventually did find him in some women's house, he would claim to be there only because he was looking after Dunky.

Apparently when Dunky went chasing women, Donnie felt obliged to go along with him to look after him and make sure he didn't get into any bother, after all look what happened a couple of years before when

Dunky ended up in intensive care, because of his womanising. So that was Donnie's excuse each and every time he was found in a strange women's house, he was looking after his wee brother, isn't that sweet.

It was going to be incredibly difficult for Donnie being hundreds of miles away, it had already been known for him to lock Annie in the house when he went out to the pub on a Friday night, he claims it was accidental, she claims it was not, I know who I believe.

They left on the fourth of January and I can't say I missed them, by this time I was back in the groove I had been in since the previous summer, I went to school then went to my friend's houses in either Mosspark or Pollokshields was home by seven thirty had whatever I could find to eat and was doing homework for the rest of the night and in bed by half ten, living the dream you could say. (If you like being sarcastic that is)

Charlie's routine was different to say the least, he spent most days trying to find a way to either not go to school or to find a way out of it once he was forced to be there. My Ma was constantly being bothered by truancy officers and was threatened several times that Charlie would be taken to a children's panel and quite possibly be taken off her and sent to an approved school, I think the reality of that finally set in and he did attend school on what could loosely be described as a regular basis.

Both Dorothy and Annie were due their latest babies in May or June, so they were well on by February and back to waddling, come to think of it, it was strange to see either of them in the past couple of years not being pregnant, they had both been pregnant by this time more than twenty months out of the last twenty five.

Darlene had blossomed into a beautiful girl who was getting far more attention from the boys than either my Ma or Da liked, Donnie before he went away to work and Dunky more recently had constantly been warning off any boys who were getting a bit too close, but Darlene was far too smart for them, she lived life to the full, I didn't know at the time what had happened in Ireland but she wasn't holding back in enjoying herself.

As soon as my Da left, our house became a teenage girl zone, every weekend there would be at least three of Darlene pals there from five o'clock on a Friday night until ten o'clock on a Sunday night. Friday night was about staying in with bottles of vodka (hidden from my Ma) and screeching about clothes, hair, makeup, boys, makeup, hair clothes and boys, in no particular order. Nothing was ever talked about everything had to be screamed at the top of a whiney annoying voice. I think the only reason my Ma put up with it was that she was relatively young and still had some things in common with the lassies, but maybe she was just fed up with the house being full of boys and boys things and there being never ending sport on the telly.

Saturday night was about dancing, specifically about going into the town centre dancing, usually at Tiffany's or Shuffles or Clouds in Renfrew street or most often the Savoy, they might try and get in to Fergie's bar at the Paisley road toll first because there was usually a band on in there on a Saturday, it just depended how much money they had scraped together between them. They would be strutting their stuff up and down our hall with their baby's dummy tits on a chain around their necks (Which Dunky never failed to tease Darlene about, since it wasn't the first time she had dummy tits) and their mixture of mini - skirts maxi dresses and bell bottomed trousers with platform heeled shoes, every weekend at least one of them got a sprained ankle either before they went out or when they were on their way home drunk.

And then there was Donny Osmond, David Cassidy, David Essex all three of them "incredibly dreamy" and appearing on giant posters on Darlene's bedroom wall, I think Alvin Stardust and Gary Glitter made an appearance as well at one point.

Her bedroom actually smelled like a pub toilet which had been sprayed with cheap perfume, there were four lassies at least living in it every weekend, drinking, smoking (mostly tobacco) and eating fish and sausage suppers in it not to mention the occasional curry or pizza, my Ma actually declared one day that she would no longer be going in to that room and if it attracted rats then Darlene could sleep with them, when Dunky pointed out it wouldn't be the first time Darlene had slept with a rat, my Ma slapped him one.

Dunky spent a bit more time in the house at the weekends, strange that really, who would have thought he wanted to stay in at the weekend in a house full of half dressed drunk teenage girls, Darlene was forever screaming at him to leave her friends alone, or screaming at her friends to stay away from him he was poison, some of them actually listened. Most of her pals referred to him as Duncan Disorderly, which he absolutely loved.

So knowing the mayhem that my house had become while my Da was away working in Corby, I couldn't quite fathom why my Ma decided to go away for the weekend to Corby to see my Da, leaving Dunky in charge and Darlene in charge of feeding us, was my Ma having a breakdown or something, fair enough leaving Dunky and Darlene in charge of Charlie and me, we could more or less look after ourselves but Paul was only six and wee David wasn't even four yet, Dunky would get them drunk or Darlene would poison them, was my Ma completely mental, was she missing my Da that much that her children didn't matter anymore.

Just before my Ma left she seen some sense and got Dorothy to take wee David, at least one of my Ma's children would probably survive the weekend.

"Cheerio Ma , enjoy yourself, don't worry about us, I will make sure the boys are alright, tell my Da I'm missing him and Donnie, ok, ok, Cheerio" Darlene was hanging out of the living room window, literally her feet were off the floor and she was very likely to go over the window sill and fall two storey's to the street below before my Ma's taxi had even left the street, actually we had a cat called Cheeky that used to fall off that window sill regularly without coming to any particular harm, she normally landed in the hedge of the bottom garden, although skinny as she was I didn't think the hedge would stop Darlene from breaking her neck, should she fall out.

I grabbed her legs and pulled her in "You're gonny go right over that ledge you half wit, if it got windy at all when you're hanging out like that you would blow away like a leaf" I shouted at her.

She kicked me in the thigh, I think she was aiming at my balls, "what the fuck is that for I just probably saved your life you stupid cow" I shouted at her again.

"Just push her out the window Danny if that's how she feels" Charlie said smiling "but try and land her in the hedge, that's what I do with Cheeky all the time, and she's alright"

Darlene grabbed him and started shaking him by the shoulders "Why would you do that to a poor wee cat, you're an evil wee bastard and I'm telling my Ma when she phones, I should pick you up and throw you into the hedge you wee shite"

But Charlie wasn't a wee shite anymore he was nearly twelve and not that much smaller than Darlene, he pushed her away forcibly and said "I'm only kidding, the cat just sits on the ledge and then falls off, everybody's seen it doing that, you've seen it doing that haven't you Danny" He turned to me.

"Aye, I have actually" I said, because that was the truth, I had seen it happen, everybody had, sometimes when I was coming home from school I would see the cat on the ledge and run upstairs as fast as I could to grab it off the ledge, Darlene herself would stand below the window and shout up until somebody came and rescued the cat, if she seen it on the ledge. So it was obviously an attempt at humour by Charlie just not a very good one.

Darlene more or less accepted that he was kidding but she said "I'll be watching you, if I see you hurting that cat I'll be telling my Ma and Da".

“Watch this” he responded, turned his back to her dropped his trousers and farted. See, that was funny, no need to make jokes about throwing a cat out of a window, just drop your trousers and loudly fart at your big sister when she’s in the middle of a strop that was awesomely funny. Paul especially appreciated that brand of humour, he spent most of the weekend dropping his wee trousers and saying “Watch this Darlene” albeit with one or two accidents. He didn’t yet have the alimentary control that Charlie had, but with some more practice he would have.

It was Friday night Darlene had promised my Ma that she wouldn’t have her friends over, she would just sit in and watch the telly after she had fed us all a nice dinner. Her friends arrived approximately eighteen minutes after my Ma’s taxi left the close. “Danny, make yous three some toast and beans and go in the kitchen all of you, the living room’s mine tonight, I’m in charge”

“My ma left you money to get us a chippy, what are you talking about toast and beans, I want a sausage supper” Charlie said belligerently.

“I want to sing a duet with David Essex, but that’s no gonny happen either, smelly arse” Darlene said skipping to open the front door and let her friends in, first in was Mags Campbell, four foot eleven tall and five foot one wide, she had electric blue bell bottom trousers on with white platform boots and a woollen jumper, which reminded me of one that my Da wore to work, in fact it might have been one my Da wore to work.

“Nice jersey Mags” Charlie offered his sartorial opinion, looking at me and crossing his eyes, Mags also had a slight turn in her left eye, Dunky said she was a stunner, the sort of stun you got when you walked into a wall and everything looked a bit strange for a minute or two.

Mags eyed Charlie with justified suspicion, she would have liked to believe that somebody was appreciating her outfit she had spent hours choosing it, but her knowledge of Charlie took over and she said “Should the weans no be in bed Darlene it’s nearly half past five”

Wee Paul walked out of the living room and said "Watch this Mags" dropped his trousers and strained unsuccessfully for a fart.

"Watch what?" Mags said mystified "Are all of your brothers mental Darlene, except Dunky I mean"

The volume got turned up full when Sally Malcolm appeared at about six o'clock, she was screechier than Darlene, sometimes it was only dogs that could hear what she was actually saying, "Oh, oh, oh who seen top of the pops last night, did you see the bay city rollers, did you see Les Mckeown" she screeched before she even got through the door. There were four of them now and they all started singing shang-a-lang, shang-a-lang. This was getting out of hand and scary.

"You told my Ma, your pals weren't coming round tonight" I said to Darlene petulantly.

"And you told her you don't drink" Mags said reaching into a carrier bag and pulling out a bottle of vodka, "Turns out your a big fat liar Darlene. All four of them squealed with laughter, I thought about how I could throw myself out of the window and make sure I missed the hedge, intensive care would be much easier to handle than this.

I dragged Charlie and Paul into the kitchen and shut the door behind me, and then made them toast and beans, I said to Paul as I put his plate in front of him "You might be better at the old farting wee man after you eat these beans," this tickled him and he started laughing so much beans were coming out of his nose, I don't know whether he had a unique connection between his mouth and his nose, but there always seemed to be something coming out of it.

The volume of screaming in the living room reached a new height and despite my serious misgivings, I went to have a look, Charlie followed me, Paul didn't he was sat on his haunches at the kitchen table trying to fart, he had eaten a full plate of beans and was determined to perfect his ability to fart at will.

I couldn't believe my eyes when Charlie and I went into the living room, there was a bay city roller there standing on the coffee table, being screamed at by Darlene and her three pals, actually it was Dunky, he had bought a pair of white trousers with tartan down the side of the legs and a white shirt with tartan down the side of the arms, he had also went and had a feathered haircut and was a dead ringer for one of the bay city rollers, Eric Faulkner I think the guys name was.

He was strutting his stuff up on the coffee table and Darlene's three pals were standing behind the couch holding their hands out and screaming as if they were at a Beatles concert or something, even Darlene was screaming, Charlie and me were killing ourselves laughing then Dunky spotted us and started pointing at us and singing shang-a-lang and gyrating on the coffee table like Tom Jones, and naturally enough as any sane person would expect the coffee table broke and he fell onto the chair next to the fire, bashing and cutting his head on the mantelpiece on the way down.

Clearly this amused everybody, why wouldn't it, Dunky whilst dancing like Tom Jones and dressed as one of the bay city rollers had fallen off our coffee table, banged his head on the mantelpiece and was currently kneeling down like a dog and shouting for someone to get him a dishtowel before the blood got all over his new white shirt. I don't deny fining it funny myself but the hilarity that Darlene and her pals were displaying was a bit over the top.

"Oh, Eric are you ok, will you still be able to make the concert tomorrow night" was Mags' sarcastic question.

"I thought it was us that should be falling at your feet Eric" Sally chipped in currently standing with her legs crossed, (do all women have bladders the size of a pea or something, pardon the pun).

The third of Darlene's pals was Ina Watson, well I say pal as far as I knew Darlene hated her, but she had appeared at the door just after Sally Malcolm pretending she was looking for somebody else and casually asking “Oh, are yous having a wee ladies night, and here’s me all dressed up with nowhere to go?” and Darlene didn’t have the heart to turn her away.

The ‘all dressed up part’ was a total exaggeration she had on a mini skirt which covered absolutely nothing, not only could you see her knickers you could almost see the waistband of her knickers, and they were a dirty washed out grey colour, but I suppose at least they were the same colour as her bra straps which could be seen through the holes in her crocheted cardigan, which she wore with only the bra underneath. Another Dunky conquest if I remember right, wasn’t he talking about her when he said “There’s no need to look at the mantelpiece when your poking the fire” I’m sure it was.

There’s a fairly good chance that poking the fire would be a lot less dangerous than poking Ina Watson, if it wasn’t venereal disease you caught it would be nits or scabies at least, how could he? And why would Darlene let her in the house, the place would probably be hoaching with fleas by the morning.

Darlene eventually took sympathy on Dunky and got him a dishtowel to wipe the blood and as she handed it to him she put a spoon down the back of his neck.

“What are you doing, you eejit, why are you putting a spoon down the back of my neck” Dunky stood up one hand holding the dishtowel and the other hand fishing down the back of his shirt trying to grab the spoon. Take that out” he shouted at Darlene.

“I’m only trying to stop the bleeding” Darlene said not happy that her genuine attempt to help was being rejected.

“That’s to stop a nosebleed you stupid bastard, my nose isn’t bleeding, I’ve split my bloody head open” Dunky said oblivious to his pun.

“What should I use for that then” Darlene asked, looking round at me, as if I would know.

“It might be worth trying a fanny pad on his head” Charlie offered as a possible solution.

Before Dunky had a chance to shout at him, Darlene in all seriousness asked “Is that what they do, do they actually stop the bleeding I thought that they just sort of sooked it up, but I suppose they must or it would never stop, I mean it’s no as if the cut heals up is it”

Even her pals looked at her as if she was an idiot, and I’ll tell you something else, there have been very few occasions where both Charlie and I were too stunned by an event or a statement to not come away with a one liner, this was one of them, how could you possibly respond to that, now, years later, I can think of one or two things maybe concerning scabs or clotted cream or something, but right at that moment I stood with my mouth open the same as everyone else.

We all had a close look at the cut on his head and the unanimous decision was that it probably wouldn’t need a stitch, Charlie offered to sew it p for him if he wanted but he might need to flatten his head a wee bit with a hammer to get it through Dot’s sewing machine. Dunky retorted that one more smart remark and Charlie was going to have more stitches than Frankenstein before the night was done.

Just at that Paul decided to join us in the living room and he said “Watch this Darlene” and he turned his back dropped his wee trousers and shit some diarrhoea down the back of his legs whilst trying for a fart.

Darlene screamed “Charlie you can fucking clean him up, that’s you that showed him that, he’s gonny be a dirty wee bastard just like you, take him ben the toilet and clean him and the three of yous get to bed you manky wee bastards, I was thirteen and I objected to being called a manky wee bastard, so as I walked past her to grab Paul and take him to be cleaned I lifted my leg and farted, “That’s how you do it Paul” I said. Charlie through his laughter said “I’m not cleaning the shite off your arse you manky bastard”

Dunky sniffed about Darlene's pals for a wee while but after his tumble from the coffee table they weren't really taking him on, except for Ina Watson, but Dunky's attitude to her was 'been there, done that' so he decided the best thing for him was to nip down to some of the pubs on the Paisley Road and let some of the talent down there appreciate his new tartan gear. Which they did I am pretty sure he met his first wife that night or perhaps the next night, it was certainly that weekend.

Midnight callers

Despite the music blaring and four teenage lassies running up and down the hall, Paul eventually got to sleep at about ten o'clock, if my ma had been here it would have been half past seven when he went to bed and he would have been out for the count by eight o'clock. Charlie and me were sitting playing cards, my Ma had recently taught us to play cribbage, so we were engrossed in fifteen for two fifteen for four etc, when we heard the door being knocked loudly, well it would need to be loudly given the current volume of Elton John and Slade which was pulsating round the house.

Seconds later Mags Campbell put her head round the door and said "Somebody at the door for you Danny"

I glanced at Charlie with a questioning look which obviously he couldn't answer, he shrugged his shoulders with an 'I don't know' gesture, and both of us leapt of the bed to find out, this was unique somebody coming to the door for us after midnight, it had to be exciting in one way or another.

It was Searcher "Is your Ma and Da still away" he asked looking furtively to the left of the front door where the stairs are.

"They only went away today Search, do you think it was a day trip to Saltcoats or something" I answered perplexed at his shiftiness, not that I hadn't seen him be shifty before.

“Come on” he said to someone who was obviously standing to his right on the stairs. And Bobby shuffled into view, I have seen a few people with sore faces in my life, in fact I’ve had them and I’ve given them I’m Glaswegian from an Irish ancestry, fisticuffs and brawling are not strangers to me in fact serious violence is also regretfully well known to me, but Bobby’s face was the worst I have ever seen and believe me I’ve seen some bad ones.

He was just a mass of cuts and bruises, Searcher or someone had obviously been trying to clean him up, the blood was smeared across his face, I hoped that this was responsible for making his face look worse than it was, it wasn’t. I dragged him into the kitchen and wet a dishcloth and started clearing some more of the blood away, both of his eyes were swollen with cuts to the eyebrows and eyelids like a boxer who had just gone ten rounds with Muhammad Ali, they weren’t black yet that would come later, there was a bruise on the side of his face that might have indicated a fractured cheek bone, his nose was still bleeding and was bent to the side, both of his lips were shredded having been smashed against his lips.

“Take your shirt off Bobby” Searcher said quietly. “There might have been part of Bobby’s torso which wasn’t bruised, but I couldn’t see it”

“Nice tits Bobby” Charlie said.

Bobby laughed and grimaced at the same time and said “Gis akis arly” I think he meant give us a kiss Charlie. “What the fuck happened to him, Search” I asked overwhelmed by the sight of Bobby’s back which was literally black and blue.

“His ma’s boyfriend, Stuart Nicol, the wanker, that’s what happened” Searcher said and he was raging, Searcher wasn’t a fighter he was a cajoler and patter merchant, he used guile and blarney to get what he wanted not violence, but there was murder in his eyes right then, and Charlie looked the same. I had marginally drifted away from Searcher and Bobby and I suppose to some extent from Charlie over the previous year or so, as I became enmeshed in secondary school with my new found circle of friends, but I could still feel the bond between them and that camaraderie included me, even if I didn't want it to.

"For fuck sake Bobby what did you do to him, this is a bit over the fuckin top is it no" I asked still trying to get the blood out of his hair, he also had a bad gash on his scalp which I hadn't noticed, I did notice some blood which seemed to be coming out of his ear, but maybe it was just running down from his scalp.

"The psycho was hitting his ma and Bobby dragged him off, they had a wee scuffle then but nothing much, Bobby isn't exactly easy to scuffle with" Searcher said.

Bobby was now six feet tall, or as Bobby himself declared when Dunky had asked him what height he was now, 'Five foot twelve'. He probably weighed about sixteen stone or so, some flab around the middle but mostly muscle, he also wasn't particularly violent he was primarily Searcher's threat of muscle, and in our age group the thought of fighting Bobby was enough to make you see Searchers point of view, he did occasionally have problems with sixteen and seventeen year olds who wanted to have a go just because of his size, but his preferred option was always to let Searcher smooth things over, but when he had to fight he could and he usually won.

"Well what happened then. Did he set about him with a hammer or a sledgehammer maybe he's in some state searcher, he looks like he's fell out a fucking aeroplane or something" I said

"Amillere" I think Bobby said "I'm still here"

"I know your still here Bobby but I don't think you're in any state to answer any questions are you, you already looked like a retard now you sound like one as well" I answered.

"A hockey stick" Searcher said.

"What" I asked, looking at him incredulously.

"He set about him with his wee sister's hockey stick, he waited to he was sleeping then grabbed the blanket off him and set about him with a hockey stick, Bobby eventually managed to get away from him and came out on to the street, I was at my window and seen him" Searcher almost whispered, there was revenge dripping from every word, each time searcher looked at Bobby, I could see his fists curl and the desire for revenge clouded his eyes and tightened his jaw.

"Why did you not phone the polis" Charlie asked.

"Because the last time the slimy bastard hit his Ma, Bobby got the polis and when they came, they told that slimy cunt too take it easy with his fists or they would have to do something about it, but they did nothing, it was just a domestic they told Bobby, and when they were away that slimy bastard told Bobby the next time he phoned the polis they would find his Ma in the Clyde, a right sweetheart eh?" Searcher said with indignation written all over his face.

I don't think any of us had ever been told that the world was fair or that life was meant to be a picnic, but this was bad, this was beyond anything we had ever had to deal with, ok I had seen covered up bruises and black eyes, on my Ma and plenty of other women, most other women actually. And I had seen boys and men take a beating, I had even seen someone hit in the face with an Irn Bru bottle, but this was bad, if Bobby hadn't been so big, and if he hadn't managed to get away he would be dead, that was how bad this was, Bobby would be dead.

"So get the polis now then" I suggested, I knew this was going to be major trouble, I didn't want to be part of it, but I knew that I would have to be, probably marginally for Bobby and Searcher, but undoubtedly for Charlie, if I didn't try and keep some sort of sanity here then Searcher was going to kill this guy, and Charlie would stand beside him and hand him the weapon to do it with. The look on Searcher's and Bobby's faces told me that they believed the polis weren't an option.

“I’ll phone them then, I’ll tell them what he done, their no gonny let him away with nearly killing a fourteen year old boy, for fuck sake their no that bad, they will lock him up” I said starting to get slightly hysterical.

Bobby had an older brother Sandy, who was in the army, “What about Sandy where is he, tell him and he’ll do the bastard” I suggested getting desperate, because I knew that Sandy hadn’t been around for almost two years, since his mother had kicked him out of the house for standing up to her boyfriend.

“eyepus” Bobby said. “Cyprus” Searcher interpreted “Has been for nine months, another year and a half to go, we need to sort this ourselves Danny, there’s nothing else for it, I’m going in the kitchen window, Bobby says it’s always left open a wee bit because of his Ma’s asthma, she likes a bit of fresh air, I’m going in the kitchen window and I’m gonny stab him, I’m going up to my house first, my Da’s got an old army bayonet in the loaby cupboard , I’m gonny go and get it and stab the bastard.” He said this with the tone of somebody telling you they were going to the co-op for some message s and they had to pop home for a message bag first.

“Can you hear yourself Searcher, are you even listening to what you’re saying, you’re gonny stab somebody, are you really, look what he done to Bobby and look at the size of you, what if he’s sitting up waiting, to see if Bobby’s gonny come back at him, what if he’s sitting up waiting with a sword in his hand or a meat cleaver instead of a hockey stick, who’s gonny get stabbed then, you, that’s fucking who, you are gonny get stabbed, gonny think about this please” I said pleadingly.

“There will be four of us even if he has got a sword, fuck him” Charlie said.

“What four of us are you talking about, Bobby, are you kidding Charlie, Bobby can hardly move, his eyes are nearly welded shut with the swelling, and you, you’re no even twelve yet, you’re a wean, he would swat you out of the way like a fly, that leaves me and Searcher, I am completely shiting myself just thinking about it and Searcher couldn't fight his way out of a wet paper bag, what fuckin four are you talking about Charlie, the fantastic four, Jesus Christ one of yous are gonny end up dead" I said sitting down beside Bobby at the kitchen table, my legs went a bit wobbly with panic.

"I'm going in the kitchen window and stabbing him, nobody needs to come with me, I'll do it myself" searcher said again in the same monotone that suggested that this wasn't up for discussion, he wasn't putting forward a plan for us to mull over and refine, as far as he was concerned he was going to do it.

Right then, do that but keep us out of it, because it's stupid, even if you do it, what then, you get the jail for ten year, no me searcher and no Charlie, we're no going to jail for a prick like that, so go ahead do it and see what happens, two choices, he kills you or you kill him and go to Barlinnie, good luck" I said with equal determination.

Searcher shook his head and walked towards the kitchen door.

"You canny tell me what to do" Charlie said petulantly.

I grabbed him by the front of his pullover with both hands and pulled him towards me and shouted in his face, "aye I fuckin can, this isn't about going to the shops or making my Ma a cup of tea you fuckin idiot, I can tell you what to do and if you take one step towards that door, I'm gonny kick your fuckin head in" That was quite possibly the only time in his life that Charlie was scared of me.

Searcher walked out without another word. We hurried into Dunky's bedroom to look out of his window which faced onto the street to see where Searcher went, including Bobby who was walking stiff legged like a zombie as well as looking like one. Searchers walked straight across the road and up his own close, presumably phase one of his master plan. After about ten minutes I was starting to feel a bit relieved , maybe he had thought better of it and just went to bed, but no he emerged from his close bundled up in what must be one of his Da's jackets, it looked like a coat on him. His hand kept going inside it, I suppose he was checking the knife was there and that it wasn't going to fall out.

This was getting ridiculous, I wanted no part of this but he was my friend, I couldn't just let him throw his life away, Charlie was beside with his face almost pressing against the glass.

"He will do it Danny" Charlie said quietly as if I doubted it for a moment.

"I know Charlie, but what can I do, I tried to stop him, he's mental, I know what this prick Nicol did to Bobby is way out of order but you canny just go about stabbing people, he should just wait and bide his time gimme time to think about it and we can maybe sort something out, but if he thinks going in like some sort of night commando is going to work, how am I supposed to stop him for fuck sake" I was actually feeling guilty about not being down there with him.

Searcher was sat on the stairs at the front of his close and he stayed there for about fifteen minutes, it was now almost two in the morning. He must have convinced himself to do it because he was suddenly up and moving towards Bobby's house.

"shit, shit, shit" I said "He's actually gonny do it, I'm going down to stop him, Charlie you stay here I mean it don't fuckin move, Bobby don't let him move ok" I was about to threaten Bobby about what would happen to him if he let Charlie move, but what could I possibly threaten him with that was worse than what had happened to him already.

I ran out the front door, the music was still going strong in Darlene's room, I couldn't understand why no neighbours had come to the door to complain, it was like a discotheque in there the music was blaring. I ran down the stairs four at a time, I was lucky I didn't break my neck. Bobby lived in a front door house right next to my close, his kitchen was at the back so all I had to do was race down the stairs out the back door of the close and turn left, I would then be right under his kitchen window, I did all that as fast as I could and I was still too late, I was only in time to see Searchers arse disappear inside Bobby's window.

I stood there, shifting my weight from foot to foot, should I go in after him, should I wait, if I go in after him I could get blamed for whatever he did in there, if I didn't I would be letting him down. As I struggled to make up my mind, Charlie came leaping out of the back close.

"Where is he" he asked breathlessly.

I heard a noise from above and looked up to see Bobby hanging out of my bedroom window making unintelligible noises, probably apologising for letting Charlie escape or shouting at Charlie for doing so.

Charlie leapt towards the drainpipe which ran down the side of Bobby's window and tried to climb it, I grabbed him before he could even get his feet up to the first joint and get any purchase.

"Where the fuck do you think you're going" I said grappling with him. Before he had a chance to respond we heard a screeching sound from inside Bobby's house and then saw searcher leap out of the window and land right at our feet. I pulled him to his feet and Charlie and I started dragging him towards our back close, as we did, I noticed he had dropped a lethal looking bayonet behind him as he had fallen, I lunged for it grabbed it and ran close behind him and Charlie into the close, all three of us flew up the stairs.

We almost got stuck in the door of my bedroom such was our haste to get in and get the door closed, Charlie collapsed onto his bed Searcher and I collapsed onto to our hands and knees struggling to catch a breath, I still had the bayonet in my hand, I tossed it under my bed.

"I rolled over onto my back and asked "What happened, what was that screeching"

Searcher was still drawing in huge lungsful of air and haltingly said "It was Bobby's cat, that slimy bastard Nicol wasn't even in, and when I was coming back out the stupid bastard cat wrapped itself round my legs and I fell on top of it, it screamed like a banshee and I shit myself and bolted."

"Inoeyawite?" Bobby asked.

"Aye, Snowy's all fuckin right Bobby" Searcher replied and we all exploded with laughter mingled with great relief.

Darlene pushed the door open and we all almost jumped out of our skin, she came into the room and slurred "Do yoush know what time it ish, the neighboursh will tell my ma" and then she staggered away again without another word. This just set us off again on an adrenalin filled burst of hilarity.

When we settled down I asked "What next then, are you gonny wait for him to come in or what?"

Searcher looked wary, "I don't know, what do you think I should do Bobby"

Bobby just shrugged his shoulders, it was probably the pain he was in and the drama of the night but Bobby looked dog tired.

"Why don't you leave it till tomorrow Searcher, let us think about it, I'm not saying that we let him away with it, but let's think before we do anything, there's no point in going to jail is there?" I said still trying to inject some reasoning into a mad situation.

Searcher shrugged his agreement, "Right we will leave it till tomorrow Danny but that bastard's getting it, one way or another, and I mean it"

"Fine, ok, I know you mean it and I agree with you but we can think about it tomorrow. Look at him he's out on his feet" I said pointing at Bobby. "You two can stay here the night if yous want, yous can both sleep in my bed, and I'll go into the bottom of Charlie's."

They agreed and we all crawled into our beds, Charlie reached up and turned the light switch, which was directly above his bed, off. After a minute or two of silence we heard Searcher whisper " For fuck sake Bobby, move over a bit this is only a wee bed, move your legs over that way and I can get on top of you"

Charlie said "Searcher, mind and be gentle with him, it's his first time and he's a bit sore" and giggled at his own joke.

I was awakened at about five o'clock after about two hours sleep by Searcher creeping about the room, "What are you doing" I shouty whispered.

"Putting my shoes on, go back to sleep" he said matter of factly as he slipped out of the room.

I got up and followed him into the living room, he was standing at the window, "look" he said holding the net curtain up and moving aside so that I could see. I looked down towards bobby's door expecting to see his wicked stepfather and my heart started to beat rapidly again.

"No, over there at the shops" he said pushing my head in the direction he was pointing.

My living room had a bay window and when standing where we were, if you looked straight ahead you would see Searcher's close two other closes and the subway station, but if you turned to the right you would see down the length of the street, to Brand street where there were a few factories, and if you turned to the left you would see to the other end of the street and across the paisley road, and across the Paisley Road were four shops in a little row, you could see those shops from my living room window.

What searcher was pointing at was two men, climbing out of a shop window with arms full of whatever it was they were stealing, it was a Pakistani corner shop, so I would imagine it was booze and fags they were nicking.

“Come on” Searcher said “Let’s see what we can get” and he was gone before I had any opportunity to object. I was standing in my vest and pants thinking, is he mad, is he absolutely mental, has he not had enough for one night, but I still went through to my bedroom and quietly pulled on a jumper and trousers and slipped my bare feet into my sandshoes and ran after him, clearly I was just as stupid as him if not more so.

By the time I got out of the close Searcher was running past me with his arms full and shouting “The polis are coming, move it”, I about turned and bolted after him, straight up my close. When we got upstairs he threw everything in his arms onto the couch in the living room and went directly to the window, I was right behind him.

The police had arrived there was just two of them no car or van so they must just have been on the beat and noticed the broken window, Searcher was lucky they were far enough away that they didn’t see him or chase him. They stood on either side of the window looking in and the one of them got on his radio, we could see him holding it up to his mouth and looking up and down paisley road west, within five minutes a police van appeared, I was thinking that maybe they were going to look for fingerprints or something, but they weren’t.

Two policeman got out of the front door of the van and opened up the back doors, the two policeman who had arrived first on foot, went into the shop through the broken window and started handing over box after box of stuff to the two van policeman who threw it all into the back of the van, in less than ten minutes the van was full of stuff and the two policemen got in and drove away.

“Dirty thieving bastards” Searcher said to me with no sense of the ironic. I laughed and said “What’s all that on my ma’s couch, searcher”

He looked at his ill gotten gains and said “Aye I know, I am a thief, but they are polis, their no supposed to steal things, their supposed to stop me from stealing things" he looked at me baffled and confused by what we had witnessed, we were both learning a lot tonight.

I walked over to the couch to examine what was there, there were twenty two packets of tomato cup-a-soup and one wee packet of Acdo washing up powder, I burst out laughing, I can't stand cup-a-soup, and I didn't fancy doing a washing in the middle of the night.

We waited up a while to see what else would happen, the answer was nothing much, Mr Patel who owned the shop arrived after about half an hour and stood laughing and joking with the two police officers and even gave them what looked like a bottle of whiskey, this made Searcher even more outraged, he wanted to tell Mr Patel what we had seen, I think he was most angry that the police had went away with a van full of goodies and all he got was a few packets of cup-a-soup, which he didn't like either. "Look on the bright said Searcher" I said "At least if Bobby's jaw is broke, and he has to eat through a straw, he's not going to go hungry is he?" and I nodded my head towards all the cartons of cup-a-soup. Even searcher smiled at that one.

Later that morning we found out that Stuart Nicol had vanished, he had taken what meagre possessions he owned and done a runner the night before, presumably just after beating Bobby. Bobby eventually found out that the reason his stepfather had been hitting his ma was that his wee sister Cynthia had told his Ma that Nicol had been trying to touch her up, Cynthia was only ten. Bobby's Ma had merely asked him what to do about what Cynthia said, she didn't believe her but wanted to know what to say to make sure she didn't say it to anybody else because Bobby's ma had ultimately decided that not only was Cynthia a lying wee cow but that her and Bobby had ruined her last chance of happiness, which was apparently Stuart Nicol, a wife beating, child beating paedophile, apparently it doesn't take much to make some people happy.

When Bobby told searcher about this Searcher said that when he went in to stab Nicol and discovered he wasn't there he had seen Bobby's Ma lying drunk on the bed, and if he had known what she was like he would have stabbed her instead, Bobby fell out with him for saying that but only for about twenty minutes until Searcher explained how selfish his ma was being and that she had actually put him and wee Cynthia in danger from that prick Nicol, Bobby relented but still told Searcher not to say anything else about his ma.

A liquid lunch.

Darlene decided since it was Sunday, she was going to make all of us a Sunday lunch, all of us being Dunky (Very hungover) Charlie, me and Paul. So she gave us an option of roast silverside of beef or chicken, which she later changed to beef as our only choice as we had no chicken. We choose beef reluctantly, we would have been happy to look after ourselves, with beans on toast or pieces and sausage. But, because it was Sunday Darlene had decided that she would show everyone what she was capable of, and she did. Personally I would have been happier to see Dunky have a go at the cooking, when he wasn't out chasing girls Dunky spent a lot of time in the kitchen with my Ma, he was actually interested in cooking, Darlene found it difficult to tell the difference between a cooker and a washing machine.

About a year previously would have been the last time she did anything in the kitchen, and that was when she blew out all of the lights and almost blew her hand off. She wasn't actually even cooking, she was drying her hair and her hair dryer blew a fuse, it was a Saturday afternoon, there was only her and Charlie in the house, she asked Charlie to do her a favour and change the fuse in her hairdryer, Charlie ignored her completely, he didn't let his eyes move from Giant Haystacks flooring Big Daddy for even a second, when she asked again, he told her not to be stupid he was busy waiting for the football results to come on, and could she do him a favour and piss off.

Darlene didn't know how to change a fuse, actually if you asked Darlene what a fuse was and where to find it on a hairdryer, the nearest you would get to an answer would be a blank stare. But she did get a butter knife and open up the plug, not because she was going to change the fuse, because she had no idea that the fuse was in the plug in the first place. No what Darlene was intending was to do was take the plug off the hairdryer altogether, and attempt to put the bare wires from the hairdryer straight into the socket on the wall, she would do this by pushing the plug from the kettle in at the same time as the two bare wires, and it worked for a few minutes until one of the wires came a little loose.

She then tried to push that in a bit further, with a fork, all the lights fused, Darlene gets blown across the kitchen and her arm ends up black from the tips of her fingers all the way up to her elbow, Charlie upon hearing the explosion and seeing the lights all go out runs into the kitchen and says "You stupid cow, the football scores were just coming on"

So none of us were very confident that she would be able to produce anything edible, in fact we were more scared that she would start a fire and burn us to death. At one o'clock she carefully wrapped the slab of silverside in silver cooking foil, when I say carefully I mean she wrapped it on like an elastic bandage, round and round she went until the foil was at least as thick as the meat, perhaps her intention was that we could play pass the parcel with it before eating it. I was assigned the task of peeling potatoes, turnip and carrots, all of which I had done before. Darlene decided that the roast would take approximately three hours so she put it in the oven at precisely half past one.

She inspected my peeled vegetables, "Those totties are too big" she said tersely.

"no they urny" I replied more tersely.

"Aye they ur" she said

"no they urny" I said, I was prepared to play the long game and say "No they urny" all afternoon if necessary"

“They ur, cut them in half” she ordered.

“No” I replied “if I cut them in half they will boil away to nothing, if you are going to mash them then I could cut them in half, but if you want whole totties then you need to leave them the size that they are” In my humble opinion I gave her this advice in a reasonable and fair manner so it came as a massive surprise when she screamed at me.

“Cut the bloody things in half, why do you always think you know everything”

“I don’t know everything, I don’t even think that I know everything but I know more than you and I especially know that they totties will be too wee if I cut them in half” I said folding my arms in finality.

She picked up the knife and cut all the potatoes in half herself. “There you go” she said “Two minutes, that’s all it took two bloody minutes”

“You’re missing the point doughball” I said, whether it took two minutes or two hours, they’re still too wee, the potatoes are undersized the totties are stunted.

“That’s a good idea “she said.

I thought for a moment or two but gave up quite quickly “What’s a good idea” I asked perplexed.

“Doughballs, we could have doughballs with our Sunday roast” she said triumphantly.

“No we canny, you can only make doughballs with mince or stew or maybe a casserole, with a Sunday roast you could do Yorkshire puddings” I said

“Same thing” she said smugly.

I was speechless, how could I continue arguing with her, I would have got a more sensible argument with the kitchen table.

"Ok" I said realising the futility of arguing with her "Will I go to the shop and get a Yorkshire pudding mix"

"What for" she asked "I thought you wanted doughballs"

"Same thing" I said and just went to the shop, my head was spinning I had to get out of there, twenty minutes with Darlene does that to you.

I was back within half an hour, I had got captured at the shop by one of the girls who worked there asking if one of the Bay city Rollers had been at my house the night before, when I told her yes, Eric Faulkner had been dancing the night away with Darlene and her pals before going to the Fountain Bar for a wee drink, I thought she was going to faint, and the look on her face was so pathetic I wondered if this could possibly be Darlene's twin sister separated at birth.

I walked slowly back to the house, dreading every step which took me closer to another conversation with Darlene, how come I got landed with her anyway, where the hell was Dunky, he liked cooking why wasn't he helping her. Having a hangover isn't an excuse, if Dunky was going to stop doing things when he had a hangover he would never do anything at all. I could hear nothing in the house when I went back in except Darlene singing to herself.

"shang-a-bang, shang-a-bang, shang-a-lang, bang-a-bang, bang-a-lang" she was screaming tunelessly.

There are only three words in the chorus of that stupid infantile ludicrous song, and they were shang-a-lang, and Darlene managed to get them wrong, I didn't correct her, it would have taken too long and been pointless anyway, Darlene makes it up as she goes along, I don't mean song lyrics, I mean everything, life in general, she makes it up on a daily basis, I swear it.

"What's that smell" I enquired when I came in the house it was now almost three thirty and Darlene had just turned on the rings under the potatoes turnip and carrots.

“What smell, what does it smell like? “Darlene asked.

“It smells a bit like roast beef, cooking away nicely in the oven” I said mischievously.

“I canny smell it” Darlene replied innocently.

I shouted at her “I know you canny smell it, because you haven’t turned the bloody oven on”

It took a few seconds but after looking at me and then looking back at the oven she said “Oh, neither I have” and she turned it on with a flourish.

“Tada there you go” she said “You don’t have to be funny or sarcastical, you just needed to turn it on.

I shook my head and said “Darlene, the roast will take at least three hours probably more like three and a half hours, which means it won’t be ready till about half past seven and the vegetables will all be ready in twenty minutes or something, now you tell me, do you think that will be a problem”

She was raging now, “No it won’t be a problem, I’ll turn the veg down, get out of the kitchen, all your doing is causing trouble, everything I do, you’re trying to make out I’m doing it wrong”

I wanted to say that was only because everything she was doing was wrong, but she never gave me the chance. “Fuck off” she screamed at me as she pushed me out of the kitchen door.

She opened the kitchen door again just after eight o’clock and shouted out “Dinners ready, come and get it”

Dunky had got out of his bed at about half past four and tried to go into the kitchen, Darlene had also told him to eff off not only that but she had also jammed a kitchen chair under the doorknob so that none of us could get in. By eight o’clock when she called us we were starving. In fact Dunky had stopped Charlie and I from going to the chippy at half past six by threatening to kick our heads in if we upset Darlene any further, it was unusual for him to support her, but she was trying I suppose.

We approached the kitchen with some trepidation, Charlie ducked behind me and pushed me forward, I jinked to the side and got behind Dunky and pushed him in first, we sat at the table and looked at our plates, on it was a piece of roast beef coal. What I mean by that was that Darlene had basically taken a piece of silverside of beef and cremated it, it was no bigger than a jammie dodger biscuit and it was black. None of us said anything for a moment or two.

"Where's the totties" Charlie asked, Darlene pointed to a jug in the middle of the table, a jug.

Dunky stretched over for the jug and poured what looked like cloudy milk unto his plate, I picked up another jug and poured some turnip over my beef, and I could only guess that the mug which was now sitting alone in the middle of the table held our liquid carrots.

"What happened, Darlene" Dunky asked gently.

"The oven was a wee bit too high" she started, Charlie opened his mouth, Dunky dug him in the side with his elbow, Darlene continued "Then when the totties were ready I added a wee bit of butter and a wee drop of milk and mashed them"
"Did you drain the water out first" Dunky asked, now struggling to suppress his laughter.

"Are you supposed to" Darlene responded. And that was it, the dam broke all three of us roared with laughter, Charlie was unable to contain himself any longer "The turnip soup, looks alright but, are they brown ball things there for dipping in the soup" he asked with tears of laughter escaping the corners of his eyes.

"That's Yorkshire puddings you cheeky bastard" she said picking up the plate and inspecting them closely "They don't look anything like brown balls"

Dunky had heard enough, Darlene was devastated that all her efforts were being so cruelly ridiculed, "Charlie, go round to the chippy and get us all some fritters and listen, you as well Danny, fun's fun but don't tell my ma about this when she gets home, as far as all of us are concerned , Darlene made roast beef and totties and it was fine, we enjoyed it, right, she tried her best now leave her alone, Dorothy will take the pish out of her if she finds out, so don't let her"

None of us had seen wee Paul coming up to the table and only noticed him when he said "Can I get more carrots" as he wiped his mouth and put the mug down on the table.

Summer of 74

There was a world cup that summer in Germany, lots of the games were on television. We watched them all, my Da Donnie and Dunky with their cans of Tennent's lager and McEwans export in hand, and Charlie trying to drain the dregs from the cans when nobody was looking. Paul watched it with us not quite sure what was happening, but getting excited when we were excited and groaning when we groaned, wee David sat propped on the couch looking from person to person and screaming with fright when we all leapt in the air to celebrate a goal or chastise the referee for blatantly ignoring Scotland's rights.

Scotland were there, we watched all of their games from the edges of our seats, and this was not only our escape but all of Scotland's attempt at escape from the harshness of three day weeks and blackouts and unemployment. There was always at least a dozen people in our living room during Scotland matches, Searcher was an ever present as was Bobby because neither of them had a television, Searchers Da hated television and said it would be the ruination of ordinary people that he thought eventually that nobody would do anything but sit and stare at moving pictures on a box, they wouldn't ever leave their seats, to run or jump or play or work or anything. He also said people were more interested in Elsie Tanner than they were in Mrs Wallis who lived in the bottom close at number six, she had recently been ill and it had been three days before anybody had noticed and gone to see what was wrong.

Bobby watched the television in our house because they didn't have one in his house, in fact they had almost nothing in his house, since Stuart Nicol had left his ma had been slowly selling off everything they owned, their house looked almost abandoned, It was a rare occasion now when Bobby would actually let any of us into his house, he would hustle us away from the front door whenever we called for him. If you did catch a glimpse it was wooden floorboards and no furniture to be seen anywhere.

The curtains of his house were perpetually closed, this was not something I noticed, I heard my Ma telling Dot on the phone that she thought Bobby and his sister should be taken into care, because their Ma wasn't looking after them anymore. My Ma was forever telling me to bring Bobby home for his tea and she quizzed him constantly "How's your Ma", "How's your sister?", "Is your brother back from the army yet?" Bobby stoically refused any meaningful answers, he would always prevaricate and give one word responses which gave nothing away. But he still kept coming back to watch the football.

Scotland performed well, really well, they could and should have done better, all they needed, all we needed, was a goal against Brazil, that was all we needed, Billy Bremner missed a golden opportunity, from all of two yards, it probably wasn't his fault, the ball came at him too quickly but he missed a chance to lift us up out of the gloom. That's more than enough about Munich '74, some things are too hard to revisit.

Bobby's ma died in August. It was never really clear what she actually died of, there was lots of speculation, lots of theories and gossip and guesses. The main one being 'the drink' how one dies of 'the drink', I'm not really sure but that seemed to be the consensus of opinion. My ma was convinced that she had just given in to depression and loneliness and gave up, because life was too hard, my Da's opinion was that she was an old soak and probably choked on her own vomit, not an opinion my Ma relished him passing on. Whatever the reason, the fact was that she was dead and Bobby and his little sister were taken into care, but that only lasted for two days because Bobby's older brother Sandy came home and it turned out he was married, he had got wed to a German girl Gretchen the year before apparently. Bobby had never told us about Sandy being married because Sandy had never told any of them not even his mother, Sandy hadn't been on an extended tour in Cyprus, Sandy had been living in the army's married quarters in Germany.

I had a conversation many years later with Sandy at Bobby's wedding , we were both a little bit under the influence of Glenmorangie and reminiscing about Cessnock street. I asked him why he had kept his marriage a secret and why he didn't come home sooner. He told me that he hated his Ma, or more accurately he hated the alcoholism that had kidnapped his ma and corrupted her into an unrecognisable monster. He didn't tell me outright that he and Bobby had been abused by one or more of her so called boyfriends, but he implied it strongly.

He did tell me of occasions where there would be five or six men sitting drinking in his living room and taking turns to go and visit his mother in her bedroom, always taking a glass of cheap wine with them, and of others who liked to 'wrestle' with the boys after they had got the mother completely pissed and unconscious. It wasn't until he was seventeen and in the army, that he understood what had been happening in that room, and then he couldn't come home, he couldn't face her or the truth of what she had become, and of what she had willingly or unwillingly condoned for the sake of a bottle of Lanliq or Old English fortified wine.

He tried to come home once and once only, by this time she was with Stuart Nicol. Sandy arrived home at one o'clock in the afternoon, he put his kit bag down in the hall walked into the living room and seen his ma sitting drunk on the couch and Stuart Nicol sitting at the fire with a drink in his hand.

Stuart Nicol asked him "did you bring a bottle with you son, we can have a wee drink and celebrate you coming home"

When sandy told him "No, I haven't brought any drink," his ma asked "What the fuck do you want then" Sandy replied "Nothing" and walked out, he never seen Bobby or Cynthia, he had no idea where they were and he reluctantly admitted he was glad he hadn't seen them because he would have wanted to take them with him and he couldn't he was seventeen.

After his mother died Sandy came home and took over her council house with his German wife, he got Bobby and Cynthia out of care and applied to leave the army on compassionate grounds, which was accepted. He became a permanent neighbour, he was considerably older than me so made little direct impact on me but he did make a significant difference to Bobby and Cynthia.

The remainder of that summer was, for me anyway, a diverse mixture of spending hot summer days in the gardens of my new found posh friends and wild weekends when my ma went to Corby to visit with my Da, this happened maybe four or five times that year. I don't think she ever found out how wild her house became within moments of her leaving for the train station. On one occasion the fire brigade were actually called on a Sunday morning, one of Darlene's pal's boyfriends had, for a dare, climbed out of our kitchen window and pulled himself onto the roof via the drainpipe. This was all very well and showed an impressive level of bravery, until it came time to come back down and he ended up clinging to the pipe with white knuckles and crying.

Charlie leaned out of the kitchen window to such a degree that I panicked and grabbed his legs, after he had kicked me away he went out on to the kitchen window ledge and told the guy on the roof to jump, it was only about fifty feet and he would be jumping on to soft grass and would probably be ok, the worst he could expect was maybe a sprained ankle, and how impressed would all the lassies be when they saw how brave he was, actually leaping a tall building just like superman.

The boy started crying harder and began accusing Charlie of attempting to murder him, I found that quite interesting, if the guy jumped and broke his neck, would Charlie be legally responsible, I didn't think so, it wasn't as if he got up on the roof and pushed him, all he was doing was standing on a window ledge mocking the guy and making him feel like a wimp and a coward, I suppose a jury might find it to be manslaughter if anything, but rather than take the chance of a prosecution I pulled Charlie in by the hair and told him to stop being an arsehole, he didn't.

Darlene dialled nine, nine, nine and asked for the police to come with a big ladder or a blow up mattress, when the operator suggested the fire brigade should come instead, Darlene rushed into the kitchen and asked if anybody had set the boy on fire, Charlie said no but if she thought it would help make the fire brigade come quicker he would do so.

The fire brigade arrived within fifteen minutes which was unfortunately five minutes after the boy recovered his composure and climbed back in the kitchen window. So when the fireman with the white hat, who I presume was the boss, started getting a bit annoyed at being called out for no reason, Charlie again offered to set the boy on fire so it wasn't a wasted journey, and if not the boy then at least the midden bins, the white hat declined and said he would get in touch with our parents when they came back, to let them know what had been going on fortunately for us he never did.

Most of the wildness of the weekends centred round Darlene and her group of pals, who enjoyed a drink or two, so you can probably imagine the type of people this attracted to our house on a Saturday night. First of all would come any other young girls aged between fifteen and twenty, even if they weren't close friends with Darlene, they would be known to her and therefore would be welcomed in like long lost family. This would in turn attract all young guys aged between sixteen and twenty five like dogs sniffing around a bitch on heat. These young guys were not as welcome as the young girls, so Dunky and his mates would be on constant alert and although it never actually came to serious physical violence, the most that ever happened was some pushing and shoving and plenty of shouted threats and obscenities.

The police were called reasonably frequently about the noise by various neighbours the remarkable thing was that none of the neighbours told my Ma and Da, well none of them made a big deal of it. I suspect my ma knew what was going on but only up to a point, but I don't think she understood that every time she went away there was a three day long party. Darlene told me years later that she thinks three of her friends and two other girls she knew of had got pregnant during those weekends, and subsequently married because of their pregnancies. So my Ma visiting my Da in Corby was actually responsible for a mini baby boom and a spate of weddings in and around Cessnock Street in 1974.

One of the girls who got pregnant was Ina Watson, and there was a good deal of speculation about who the father might have been. Dunky was definitely in the frame, for a month or two until it was revealed by Ina Watson that she hadn't actually had intercourse with Dunky for months, they had 'done other things' but not intercourse. She was in fact pregnant by her older and recently married first cousin, this wouldn't be revealed until about two years later, when she got pregnant by him again and they ran away together to live in a housing scheme in Kilmarnock, I think it was called Onthank Estate or something like that, which they must have imagined was far enough away to hide from the shame.

August and September 1974 also seen the arrival of two new grandchildren for my Ma and Da, Annie gave birth to her third child and second son Duncan junior, and Dorothy gave birth to her third child and second son Christopher named after his paternal grandfather. Both of them entered the world and our family with remarkably little fuss, well remarkably little fuss for us. Christopher did decide to make his appearance during a subway ride but as luck would have it the subway train was just pulling into the Govan station (which is and was very close to the hospital) just as Dorothy's water's broke. So rather than wait for an ambulance the man in charge of the station took Dorothy to the hospital in his own car which was a two seater red sports car, Dorothy was delighted and would probably have liked some photographs of the occasion, Tony was jealous and threatened to go down and kick the guys head in.

Away days and boat trips

The best thing about that year was that with regular work coming in, and in particular out of town work which paid substantially more money, my Ma and Da were able to get back on their feet financially and clear off the bills which had left us in the dark, not only that but there was even cash for extras. Such as my Da buying a van.

"You must be joking" I said, as I stood beside my Ma and Darlene looking out of the living room window and seeing my Da getting out of a ford transit van at our close. To say the van had seen better days would have been an understatement of massive proportion, it was a wreck.

It did have four wheels, albeit one of the rear wheels looked bigger than the other three, it was presumably meant to be blue, but the patches of rust on it were so big that it looked like a blue and brown cow with wheels. There was a crack the length of the windscreen and one of the panes of glass in the back doors had been replaced with a sheet of plywood. You couldn't get into the driver's seat via the driver's door because it had been welded shut for some reason, you had to go in through the passenger door and climb over the gearstick, which conveniently was lower than it should have been because it was falling through a rust hole in the floor. Only one of the back doors opened, actually that's not strictly true but when you opened the left hand door it fell off, because one of the hinges had been eaten away with rust, so technically you could open that door but you would then have to lift it off the ground and put it back on. Apart from all of that it was a lovely van.

Its primary purpose was to take my Da and Donnie back and forward from Corby, it didn't look capable of making it back and forward from the end of the street if you ask me. But what did I know about vans, this monstrosity actually took us up and down the west coast of Scotland to Saltcoats, Stevenston and Ayr on a regular basis for a couple of years, it was fantastic not only did it take us, it also took several of our friends and neighbours, it was rare on a trip down the west coast to have less than twelve people in the back of that decrepit old van.

Sure we had to push it sometimes to get it moving, but then we had to push my Da sometimes to get him moving as well. Charlie would brave the water no matter the temperature, I would wade in occasionally when the sun was out, Paul and wee David were as adventurous if not more so than Charlie.

"Where did you last see them Danny" My ma asked from beneath her sun visor. My Da had brought home a dozen sun visors, from god knows where. My Da had a tendency sometimes to turn up with the strangest of things at times and declare that he could make something useful out of that. Actually these visors looked more like what you would see a blackjack dealer wearing in a casino, but they were excuse enough for all of us to organise a day out to Ayr to try them out.

"I don't know ma, I was down in the rocks collecting whelks and looking for mussels, it's been ages since I saw them, I thought they were up here with you and my Da" I said apprehensively, Charlie, Paul and wee David hadn't been seen for a while and I absolutely knew this was about to become my fault.

"Aye the boys were up here with us Maggie, Danny went down to the rocks a while back, and the boys were here with us after that" my Da amazingly rescued me from the blame.

"Well, why were you no playing with them anyway" my Ma said, determined to find a way to blame me, it appeared.

My Da started laughing "Damned if you do Danny son, damned if you don't. They will be about here somewhere, if I know Charlie, he'll be trying to find a way to nick some ice cream or candy floss, from one of them stalls up at the main road, I'll take a walk along and look for them. They won't have gone that far, they're only somewhere along the beach, what's the worst that could have happened"

Before he took even one step we seen a police car stop above us on the road adjacent to the beach, when we all turned to look at it the first thing we saw was a policeman getting out of the front seat and holding the back door open to let Paul get out. He immediately ran to my ma and jumped into her arms, Paul I mean, not the policeman.

He was sobbing, it was a few minutes before his panicky sobs became anywhere near coherent, "Charlie widnae let me in the boat, he said I was a pain in the arse ma, and he widnae let me in the boat with him and Davie, I want to go in the boat" the last part was a wail.

"What fuckin boat" my Da said turning and staring at the policemen as if they had done something wrong.

"Apparently two young boys, one approximately twelve years old and a toddler were seen getting into a little rowing boat along at the harbour and then they rowed away, the coastguard has been alerted and they are looking for them now." The policeman who said this glanced at my ma and then gestured to my Da to apparently walk out of hearing distance so as he could tell him something else, not a good something else I would have thought.

"Stay where you are Davie, say what you have to say son, don't try to protect me from bad news, that's just about all I get" my ma said with a tremor in her voice.

"It's not bad news as such missus, I was only going to say that a lot of the fishing boats in the harbour are away out to look for them as well because that bit of water just outside the harbour is really choppy and two weans could be in a lot of bother if that's where they rowed to, but I'm sure they never went that far, they probably rowed fifty yards and then got pushed back on to the beach, we will probably find them at the crazy golf course or something. A twelve year old would have to be really strong to get more than a hundred yards off shore when the tides coming in, and not only that he would have to be a determined wee bugger as well"

My ma could only shake her head as she glanced at my Da and me, she never said it but we could see on her face, if the policemen wanted to meet a twelve year old with enough determination and strength to do whatever he wanted to do, he just had to meet Charlie.

I thought fair enough if Charlie wants to copy wee Jinky Johnstone the Celtic footballer who got lost out to see quite near here not so long ago then hell mend him, but what on earth possessed him to think it was a good idea to take wee David with him, David was barely four year old for god's sake.

My da asked the policemen what we could do to help, he was told that somebody should remain where we were beside the bags of sandwiches the tartan flasks and the bottles of Irn Bru and Strike Cola which constituted our lunch on the beach, in case the boys wandered back of their own accord, and anybody else who wanted to could walk along the beach road and look in the various amusement arcades and cafe's for any sign of the boys.

One police officer then suggested that he remained on the beach with my ma and my Da and I could go with the other policeman in the car and he would drive us about looking for the boys. My Da to his credit said "You don't need both of us in the car, Danny you go with him son and I will stay here and look after your ma"

I turned to my Ma expecting her to be frantic, she wasn't, not really, initially there was a panic stricken look in her eyes but that was quickly replaced with a look of resignation, as if this drama was to be expected, perhaps she was right, wherever Charlie turned up, high drama usually followed. She said "Charlie has got a dark blue jumper on Danny and his denims, wee David has got a white T-shirt with Scooby Doo on the front, and blue shorts."

I said "I know" and walked away with the policeman. He told me to get in the back of the car, I wasn't allowed in the front, as he opened the door and I squeezed past him into the back seat I could see people on the other side of the road openly staring at me and wondering what I had done to be arrested at3 o'clock in the afternoon, and incredibly, I felt guilty, just for getting into a police car. I have no idea why I should have felt guilty I had done absolutely nothing wrong, unless of course you wanted to consider my Ma's question earlier as to why I hadn't been with my brothers in the first place, as if my absence made it excusable for Charlie to be a dickhead.

The policeman drove slowly along the beach road, coming to a complete stop when we were approaching groups of boys or even boys of appropriate ages by themselves. He must have seen the worried look on my face as he scanned his rear view mirror because he said "They will probably be alright son, like my pal said, they won't have gone far, the tides starting to come in and getting out beyond the sand banks about two hundred yards offshore, isn't easy, it isn't easy at all and then there's the rip tide" he looked embarrassed somehow when he said that and stopped speaking, fortunately I had no idea that a rip tide was a current found near any shore between sandbanks which looked calm on the surface but apparently dragged unwary people on the water out to sea very quickly.

We reached the end of the beach road and the policeman asked me "Should we had back along the other way, or should we look in the town centre maybe, what's your wee brother like, would he be in the arcades do you think or would he go looking for mischief in amongst the shops and that"

I laughed inwardly, how could I answer that question, what is your wee brother like, I had a grin stuck on my face when I thought actually mister if you want to find Charlie just ask yourself one question, where is the worst possible place he could be and look there. I answered "Charlie will be out in the water in a rowing boat, probably headed for Ireland or if he thought he could get away with it, he would bypass Ireland and head straight for America"

The policeman smiled indulgently thinking I was joking or being ridiculous, but I think the look on my face convinced him that perhaps we were looking in the wrong place. His police radio which was on a strap at his shoulder started crackling and he held it up to his ear to hear better. He looked in his rear view mirror again and turned his radio all the way down quite quickly and nervously.

"I'm not hard of hearing or hard of thinking" I said. The person on the radio had said that an empty rowing boat had been found about two miles along the beach at the bottom of some cliffs but there was no sign of any children and asked all 'units' to make their way to the location.

"Can you take me along there with you" I asked.

He pondered this for a moment or two and said "I better not son, I will take you back to your ma and da and see what they want to do with you, I think"

"Why, so I can stand and watch my Ma crying or my Da getting angry because there's nothing he can do, take me along to the beach and let me help look for them, you never know they might be hiding somewhere scared, if they are and wee David sees me he will come out straight away, if he sees some big ugly polis, no offence, he's going to stay right where he is, so let's move our arses before it gets dark" I said trying to smile and look calm.

He looked at his watch and said "It's just turned four o'clock, it doesn't get dark to after ten o'clock, so what are you talking about"

I smiled again and said "I know but the speed you were driving up beach road it might take us hours to go two miles, and anyway it sounds a bit more like the Sweeney if you put some urgency into it, rather than Dixon of Dock green, I mean."

He gave me a funny look, as if I shouldn't be joking whilst something so serious was unfolding around us, but what did he think I should do, wail and cry hysterically, I would leave that to Darlene if you don't mind. It's immensely better to laugh when you're facing disaster, it covers up the fear and terror a lot better than crying.

He walked away and turned his back to me and got on his radio, I couldn't quite hear what was being said, but he appeared to be putting up an argument for whatever it was he was asking for.

"Right, in the car, we are going to along to where the boat was found and help them search for your brother's I just had to argue with my sergeant so I could bring you along, so don't be a wee shite when we get there, stay where I can see you, if you go missing my sergeant will cut my balls off with a rusty spoon, and that's not to say what your ma will do to me, or your Da." He said, already I think, beginning to regret including me in the search party.

"I swear big man, I swear on my Ma's grave I won't do anything wrong, I'll stay beside you all the time. It'll be like me and my wee shadow, Hank Marvin won't have a look in, I'm telling you" I said moving towards the car and opening the back door.

As he climbed into the driver's seat he looked over his shoulder and said "What do you mean you swear on your ma's grave your ma's no dead, I just met her half an hour ago"

"I never said she was dead big man, but she said she wants to be buried beside her ma, so in a way her grave already exists, do you know what I mean" I said smiling yet again, as he pondered this latest bit of nonsense I was spouting I added "And it might be an idea if and when we see my Ma that you don't look as shit scared as you did when whoever it was on your radio told you about the boat"

It only took us ten minutes to reach the place the boat had been spotted it was on the beach at the bottom of what I suppose could be called a cliff, but it was maybe only about forty feet high, it actually looked a bit like one of those white cliffs of Dover in miniature, it seemed to be just a big wall of sand with some grass at the top. When we arrived, there was already an ambulance, a fire engine and two police van's, all pulled up in a lay-by at the top of the miniature cliff. The guys who had been driving all these vehicles seemed to be standing about talking to each other, with a couple of them pointing down at the beach, presumably at the rowing boat which was lying upside down in the sand.

We scrambled down a pathway onto the beach and made our way over to the upturned boat, which looked like a heap of deadwood that might have been there for decades.

"How do they know that's the rowing boat that Charlie and Paul were in" I asked my new best friend the policeman.

"Because of the name on the side" he said with a look on his face that suggested, he couldn't decide whether I was a chancer or an idiot, or perhaps a bit of both "The Titanic" he added.

"What?" I asked and then noticed the name scrawled on the side of the boat.

"Somebody with a sense of humour" he suggested and smiled at me.

"Why?" I asked, completely unaware of the name.

"The Titanic" he said "You know the big boat that sank, years and years ago"

“Never heard of it” I said “and anyway what’s so funny about a boat sinking, what kind of cruel sense of humour is that to call your wee boat after a big one that sunk, that’s sick if you ask me, no funny at all, did anybody die on it, big man?”

“My Name’s PC Gilmartin not big man and aye quite a few people drowned, it was all a bit of a scandal at the time“ he said starting to look a bit guilty that he had started down this line.

“So run it by me again big man, you’ve got a wee rowing boat and a tin of paint, what’s so funny about naming that wee boat after a big boat that sank and killed a lot of people, is that no a bit jinxy as well as sick, but you seem to think it’s funny, I’m starting to worry about you pc Gilmartin, I hope if anything’s happened to my wee brothers, you’re not going to be trying to turn it into another wee joke, with your sick sense of humour”

He looked at me with horror, he might have had a sense of humour but he didn’t really get Glaswegian sarcasm in the face of tragedy, if you ask me. As he was trying to think of a way out of the quandary I had placed him in, there was a little bit of commotion further along the beach, I could see a policeman pick something up and wave it in the air.

“What is that he’s waving” PC Gilmartin asked.

“It looks like a sandshoe” I answered “Wee Paul had sannies on, maybe they think it’s one of his”

The policeman who had picked up the sandshoe walked towards me and asked “Could this be your brothers” as he held out a black sandshoe.

“Are you kidding” I asked him incredulously “There’s probably a thousand weans walking about here with them on, look” I gestured at my feet and my sandshoes “Or maybe you want me to smell it and see if I recognise his smell” I added with derision.

At least he had the manners to look embarrassed at his own stupidity. All of the people on the beach spread out and started searching again, I thought to myself that I hope they don't find a white tee shirt because that would prove it beyond reasonable doubt, I mean surely Paul was the only child in the whole of Ayrshire who was wearing sandshoes and a white tee shirt, buffoons.

PC Gilmartins radio crackled into life again, after a few seconds he looked worriedly at me, but I had heard what he had and there was no point in him pretending otherwise.

"It might be a mistake" he said "People make mistakes like that all the time, it might be nothing at all" he said completely unconvincingly.

"So what part of, somebody has reported a body under the legs of the pier, do you think might be a mistake big man" I asked, bursting into tears, at least that let him know my sarcasm could only hold me for so long.

He put an arm awkwardly round my shoulder and guided me back up the path we had descended towards his panda car, when his radio once again crackled a message full of static.

"False alarm, it's a white tee shirt and a co-op carrier bag in the water" was the message.

We both laughed him with relief and me with embarrassment at the tears running down my face unnecessarily. I sat in the back of the Panda car crying, whilst PC Gilmartin stood outside speaking to his colleagues who all seemed to cast sympathetic glances in my direction, I'm not sure why I was crying at this point because I was one hundred per cent certain that nothing had happened to either Charlie or Paul. It may just have been the tension of the moment I suppose, it didn't take long for me to recover my composure and wind the window down.

"Big man, can you take me back to the arcades and we will look there again, if Charlie is anywhere it will be there" I suggested, PC Gilmartin looked towards another policeman who had fancy braiding on his hat, who nodded and turned his back on us.

The look on his face told me he was glad to be away from the guy with the fancy hat, and I think I heard him mutter, arsehole, under his breath but maybe not.

“So why do you think Charlie is likely to be at the arcades has he got money to play the machines” PC Gilmartin asked me.

“Probably not” I replied “But that won’t stop him, he will either try to bump with his arse the penny cascade machines that spill two pence pieces down the side or he will stand beside some wee boy telling him how to play a machine and demand a cut if he wins, Charlie doesn’t need money to play in the arcades neither do I” I suddenly realised who I was talking to and further realised I had grassed on Charlie.

PC Gilmartin laughed “That’s exactly how I used to do it” he said “And another thing, the cascade machines sometimes just randomly spit out money, so it’s always worth checking all of them for anything that’s dropped into the payout tray by itself”

“I know, you can just be standing there and hear a bundle of two pence’s come pouring out and you’re swivelling about trying to see which machine it’s coming from and then it’s a mad race to get to the money first.” I said, getting into any kind of conversation was better than thinking about where Charlie and wee Paul might be, they had been gone for a few hours now and my feeling of confidence that they would turn up was beginning to reduce by the minute.

I don’t know if PC Gilmartin could see this thought in my eyes or being a policeman gives you a kind of sixth sense but he said “They will be alright wee man, when it’s something really bad you usually find out really quick, bad news doesn’t take it’s time son, not usually anyway”

A couple of tears escaped me, as I wiped at them with my already wet sleeve I replied “Don’t call me wee man, my names Danny”

His Radio sparked into life yet again but this time we both laughed out loud, apparently Charlie and David had been found. They had been underneath the shed at the beach that sold candy floss, ice cream and confectionary.

Later when asked why they were under there it emerged that they had abandoned the rowing boat barely ten minutes after getting into it because it was too hard to keep it straight, so they just jumped out on the beach and pushed the boat back out into the water to 'see where it would go '.

Charlie then told everybody that David had initially crawled under the ice cream hut because he spotted a ten pence piece shining in the sun just out of his reach which had clearly rolled under the shed, when he crawled under he whispered to Charlie that there was loads of money and he should join him under there, so Charlie did. Apparently as people were standing buying their ice cream or candy floss if they happened to drop any change it sometimes rolled out of reach under a kicker board at the bottom of the shed, so Charlie and David in fact found almost two pounds when they first went under, but while they were under the shed three more ice cream buyers dropped money which ended up in Charlie's hands. So obviously Charlie decided that it was worthwhile staying under there for a while, so they did, for about an hour.

They then came out and went to the arcades and spent their found money and when it was finished decided to sneak back under the shed and await more manna from heaven, a good idea on the surface until they both fell asleep that is. Having slept for a few hours and woke up to no more cash whatsoever they gave up and went back to the beach to find everybody else, having no idea that they had been missing for four and a half hours.

Everyone was caught in a mixture of relief, amusement and anger, obviously the bulk of the relief was felt by my ma, everybody seen the funny side and the anger was primarily mine and my Da's. He was angry presumably because he had felt impotent whilst they were missing, unable to find them and unable to promise he could sort this problem, a father's worse nightmare, he had seen it as his responsibility to keep us safe and he had almost failed. But a considerable portion of the anger was mine, yet again Charlie had ruined it for everybody, he was the centre of attention yet again, the focus of everybody and nobody seemed to realise that without his antics we could have all have had a pleasant and enjoyable day at the beach.

Instead of which we had another day of Charlie induced drama, now that he and David had been found everybody was laughing and joking about where they were and what they had been doing, and the laughter tinged with relief brought smiles to all of their faces, not mine, I wanted somebody to grab him by the throat and slap him for spoiling everybody's day ,or at least acknowledge that he had ruined our day out, but that wasn't going to happen, this would just be another amusing incident to reminisce over in the future, do you remember the day Charlie went missing at the beach, ha ha ha. When it should have been, do you remember Charlie's total selfishness in ruining everybody's lovely day at the beach, but it wasn't the first time he had been utterly selfish and it would certainly not be the last.

Chapter nine

Boys to men

It was the end of the summer and the night before we went back to school, I was sitting at the kitchen table with Donald and Duncan, I think this was probably the first time in my life I engaged in an actual conversation with them.

"Your fourteen now Danny, time to start being a man, I got my first job on the milk floats when I was fourteen." Donald said dipping his Rich Tea biscuit into his cup of tea.

"I started work two days before my fourteenth Birthday Danny, remember on the Alpine ginger lorries, I loved that, and if I hadn't gave away as many bottles of ginger to all the lassies, I would probably be a driver by now." Dunky said with a wistful sigh.

Donnie and I looked at each other and laughed "You couldn'y drive a dodgem you eejit, if you weren't looking at the lasses on the pavement instead of watching the road, you would probably be drunk anyway, you would be a crash waiting to happen" Donald said laughing.

"He is right Dunky" I added seeing Dunky's surprise at Donnie's assessment of him "you spend three quarters of your time drunk and the other quarter of your time chasing birds, I think you and a driving licence should always be strangers to each other, I wouldn't trust you pushing a pram on the pavement."

Even Dunky nodded his head and laughed when he said "You might be right Danny, I'll just let you and Charlie pick me up from the town, when I'm drunk then"

Up to this point I had always seen Donald as something like a second father, he had been working since I was four years old, so I didn't perceive him to be a brother at all, he was an adult, I was a child, so it surprised me when he said "I don't mean get a job to be a man Danny, your too good at school to be leaving at fourteen and starting some shitey job and drinking your wages down the Paisley road, I mean start being a man by getting your act together and deciding what you want to do with your life, don't get stuck with what all the no users about here have, stick in at school and rise above them" he took another sip of his tea and kept his head down as he spoke.

I am positive he wasn't talking about himself, from what I could see he was reasonably happy in his life, he had the baby machine Annie spitting out a wean every year, and they seemed to fight less than most people, although there were the few times when Annie went hunting for him in the middle of the night that he probably didn't enjoy his lifestyle, but generally he seemed to be ok with things. He couldn't be talking about Dunky, because he was as happy as a pig in shit, he had a different lassie just about every weekend and none of them seemed to mind that he was drunk ninety percent of the time he was with them, although he had recently been seeing a lassie called Elaine from Govan more often than not.

"I've no intentions of leaving school Donald, and just in case you didn't realise it I couldn't even if I wanted to, the school leaving age is sixteen now, whether I like it or not, I'm stuck in school for at least two years, and probably more really, because I will probably stay on and go for my highers if I do ok in my O-levels next year" I said, not yet realising that this was an actual conversation with Donald and Dunky, not carrying on or pretend fighting or hurling soft abuse at each other, a real conversation. When I did actually think about it sometime later, I thought that perhaps that was the precise moment I stopped being a boy and started the transition to being a man.

Dunky, being Dunky brought the conversation down to his level "Anyway Danny, if you stay on at school there's a much better chance of losing your virginity, because it's mostly birds that stay on at school, so if there's a shortage of boys, you might find one or two of the uglier lassies feeling sorry for you and letting you ride them"

Both of them burst out laughing, probably at how red my face had become, or at the look of horror I directed at Dunky, no way was I going to discuss sex with them, so I tried to stammer my way to changing the subject, "I'm no, no, no like you Dunky, I wouldn't just go with anybody just for the sake of it, I'm more choosy, and anyway I'm too busy trying to get into the rugby team to be bothered with lassies" maybe if I hadn't been so flustered I wouldn't have said it quite like that.

Both Donald and Dunky were now almost pishing themselves they were laughing so hard, Donald managed to splutter through his snotters and tears "And what one of the rugby team do you want to get into the most, I'll bet it's the hooker"

"yous two are a couple of pricks" I shouted at them as I left the kitchen with tears in my eyes, "Arseholes" I shouted as I slammed the bedroom door behind me and threw myself onto the bed, raging at my mouths inability to say what I meant it to say when I meant it to say it, because what I meant to say, in fact, it doesn't matter what I meant to say, they were a couple of pricks and that's that.

I avoided them for the next few days because every time I did see them they would pretend to get in a scrum position and start pretend kissing each other, they weren't only a couple of pricks they were a couple of weirdo's as well, arseholes.

I probably shouldn't have had a laugh at Dunky's predicament when we were all sitting in the kitchen waiting for my Ma to put out our dinner when he told her that, Elaine the girl from Govan was pregnant and that they were getting married. Donny who wasn't there for his dinner but had come up to give my ma a few quid which he did most weeks just to help her out when he could, burst out laughing and said "you told me last week that you couldn't stand her and you were trying to dump her but she wouldn't take the hint"

Dunky looked a bit shaken when he replied "That was last week, this week she's pregnant and we are getting married"

My Ma didn't seem to think that this was particularly funny and she said to Donny, "what are you laughing at, I can still remember Annie's wedding dress being quite far out at the front even if you canny, and Dunky of course yous are getting married, but I think maybe you should be bringing the lassie here for us to meet her first what do you think?"

I couldn't resist it "Would it not be better Ma if you just met her at the wedding, we could have a big dramatic moment when she lifts up her veil and we can all see how ugly she is at the same time" I said and laughed, nobody else did.

"you wee bastard" Dunky said rushing round the table at me, Donny managed to stop him from seriously hurting me, but he did get a few kicks and punches in before I even had a chance to retaliate, Charlie, as usual, weighed in on my side and started throwing punches at Dunky.

My ma screamed "Enough, enough, Charlie stop trying to punch Dunky this has got nothing to do with you, Charlie stop it right now"

Charlie paused for breath but it was my ma that stopped him throwing punches, by grabbing his hair and dragging him almost under the table, before screaming at him to stop fighting.

My Ma was still shouting "Danny that's a horrible thing to say to your brother, apologise right now and Dunky if you call any of your brothers a bastard again, it's me that will be punching you" she turned back to me and said "Danny I told you to apologise right now or you can get to your bed with no dinner"

I looked at Charlie first and smiled, then I looked at Dunky and said "Ok, I'm sorry, I'm really sorry that you've got an ugly bird" and again I laughed, this time Charlie laughed with me, my Ma didn't, she grabbed me by the neck of my shirt and pulled and pushed me into my bedroom while raining down slaps at any part of me I left exposed, I did my best to prevent excess brain damage by wrapping my arms around my head.

I'm not very tall but when I was fourteen I was already six inches taller than my Ma and about two stone heavier, so how come she had ten times my strength and could slap harder than Dunky could punch, I didn't understand it then and still don't.

As she dragged me down the hall towards the bedroom the front door opened and Darlene came into the hall, she looked at my Ma dragging me along and slapping me and asked Charlie "What's the matter, what's he done this time"

Charlie presumably was about to tell her the full story, but when he said "Dunky's girlfriend is pregnant" Darlene interrupted him and screeched "What the one from Govan, Oh Danny how could you get her pregnant, she's not even that good looking"

My Ma stopped slapping me for a minute to try and digest what Darlene had said and she shouted at Darlene "Danny never got her pregnant you half wit, Dunky did"

Darlene looked puzzled and said "Well I don't think it's fair that your hitting Danny if it was Dunky that got her pregnant, how is that Danny's fault, how was he supposed to do anything about that, sometimes I think this whole family is mental, is the dinner out yet" as she flounced past Charlie and Dunky who were stood speechless at the kitchen door.

I think my ma was too flummoxed by Darlene to remember that she had been in the middle of beating me black and blue, I slipped out of her grasp and slipped into my bedroom, but I gave the door a good slam to make a point, I'm not sure now which point I was trying to make, but I probably did then.

About an hour later my Ma came into my bedroom with a plate of fish fingers, chips and beans, which was probably lovely about an hour before when she put it in the grill to keep it warm, but was now rock hard fish fingers and chips with dehydrated beans.

"Here, see if you can eat any of this, Danny at some point in your life son, you need to realise that the first thing to come into your head shouldn't always be the first thing to come out of your mouth, you might think it's funny or clever but it isn't always. Sometimes it's cruel and sometimes it's hurtful, when you feel a desperate need to say something try and make it be something nice, you've got the sense to do that Danny, so don't be hurtful with that mouth of yours eh son" she said with a weary look on her face. "You are clever Danny and you can be really funny, but don't use your cleverness to hurt people Danny, I'm sure Dunky's girlfriend isn't ugly and you were trying to be funny, but he's trying to take in that the lassie is pregnant and his whole life is gonny change as of right now, so maybe he didn't get your joke, so use the brains I know you've got and at least try to be careful what you say in future"

I didn't realise it then, probably none of us did, but she knew me in fact she knew all of us better than we knew ourselves, it was little glimpses of her like this that I later realised was undeniable proof of the depth of her love for all of us. She expressed that love all the time with kisses and cuddles and describing us as her handsome boys and beautiful girls. But what none of us realised until we were much older was that not only did she love us, but she loved us even when she knew absolutely everything about us, she knew that we were capable of bad things as well as good, she was the one that tidied up most of the messes we created with our stupidity or naïveté or just maybe when we were being rotten and bad, but however evil or stupid we were capable of being she loved us unconditionally and completely.

Dunky brought his girlfriend Elaine to our house that Saturday night, it wasn't a party as such it was just the normal couple of hours of continued drinking after the pubs shut by my Ma and Da, Donnie, Dot and Tony, Dunky was the latest to join this group drinking away their Friday and Saturday nights in the Campden bar at the Paisley road toll, and to be fair she wasn't ugly.

This had been a recent development for my Ma in particular, my Da had always spent two or three nights a week in the pub, but it was only in the last few months probably since she had went to Corby with him, she had got a taste for the lifestyle he was living I suppose. I don't remember her having a drink when I was younger a couple of glasses of sherry at the New Year maybe, but the culture in our house was now centred round Friday and Saturday nights in the pub.

Saturday and Sunday mornings had now become ritualised as well, if my Da wasn't working the weekend he would be there on a Saturday morning sitting up in bed propped up by pillows, with his glasses on reading the sports pages of his daily express and writing out his betting slips for the day, my Ma would be in the kitchen doing the weekend fried breakfast for him and probably rolls and sausage for all of us. Saturday afternoons would normally be spent in front of the telly watching The World of Sport including watching whatever horse racing was on to see if my Da's bets had come up, because when they did all of us benefitted, there was always a couple of quid for everybody that was there, but more importantly it put my Da in a good mood and reduced the chances of him and my Ma fighting when they came back from the pub.

It seems to me that he did actually win something reasonably regularly, he put this down to being rewarded in some way for his honesty. Whilst on his way to the betting shop one Saturday morning he had found a wallet, it turned out this wallet had over a hundred pounds in it, but it also had the owners name and address, my Da went to the guys address and returned his wallet with the money intact, the grateful owner gave my Da a fiver reward and my Da claimed that he used that fiver to place his bets that day and won two hundred pounds.

For years afterwards whenever he had a win in the bookies he would claim it was because of his honesty that day, when I asked him if he thought that on all of the Saturday's that he didn't win did he think he was being punished for some act of dishonesty in the past, he told me to shut up and don't be stupid, that was just down to bad luck or crooked jockeys.

Early Saturday evenings were a buzz of activity, normally we would all be gathered there. My Ma Dot and Darlene would all be jostling for position at the various mirrors in the house getting ready to go out, Donnie Dunky and my Da would be having a can of lager in the living room watching the football results come in and checking their Littlewoods pool coupons. Charlie and I would be despatched to the chippy, depending on whether my Da had won in the bookies that day or not it would either be bags of chips for everybody, or fish suppers for my Ma and Da and sausage suppers for the rest of us, except Darlene who swore blind that chips were bad for your complexion so she would have fritters instead. There was a period between six and seven O'clock where there would be frenetic activity, with six or seven people all trying to get dressed or doing last minute ironing, Dunky was especially prone to this.

"Ma where's my good shirt" Dunky would say as he emerged from the bathroom having washed and dried his recently feather cut hair.

My Ma would shout back "Where did you last see it Dunky" whilst she moved Darlene out of the way of the mirror hanging in the hall so as to apply the finishing touches to her lipstick.

"On the room floor last Sunday probably" Dunky would answer facetiously.

"Well maybe you should look there then" My Ma would answer just as facetiously, whilst Darlene tried to edge in to use the same mirror my Ma was using. "Darlene will you get away from me, I'm trying to fix my face and you keep crowding me, what are you doing putting make up on anyway, you're watching they four tonight" They four being Charlie, Paul David and me.

"She's no watching me" I would protest, "I don't need a babysitter, especially one as stupid as her, you would be safer just putting me out on the window ledge and giving me some razor blades to play with" I added.

"She's no watching me either" Charlie chipped in, "I'm going out tonight"

"No you're not" my Ma said to Charlie, you will be staying in and helping your sister look after the weans.

"I don't think so" he responded "And if I am then that will cost you, I'm not an unpaid babysitter"

As my Da walked out of the living room and heard this he said to Charlie "And any more of your lip and it will cost you a sore arse, if your Ma says you're staying in then you're staying in"

"Ma, seriously where is my good cheesecloth shirt I'm meeting a bird in the Jester at seven o'clock" Dunky said in a pleading voice.

"It's washed and in one of your drawers go and bloody look for it and stop your greeting" my Ma said to him before adding "and you can bloody well iron it yourself, you've had all day to get bloody ready so don't start whining at me, and what do you mean you're meeting a bird, your engage to Elaine"

"Aye Ma engaged no married, Darlene go and get that shirt and iron it for me and I'll give you fifty pence" Dunky pleaded with Darlene.

"Stick your fifty pence up your Jacksy and do your own ironing" was Darlene's response,

"I'll do it" I said, fifty pence was fifty pence after all.

"All right" Dunky said "I'll give you twenty pence for doing it then"

"You just said you would give her fifty pence" I said indignantly.

"I know" he replied "but she knows how to iron it right and you don't"

I thought about it for a moment and replied "Well stick your twenty pence up your Jacksy beside Darlene's fifty pence then and iron it yourself, you look like a poof with that haircut and your cheesecloth shirt on anyway"

"I'll iron it for ten pence" said Paul.

"You canny iron it ya eejit your only six" I said to Paul

"So what" he replied "why don't you mind you own business, I nearly got ten pence for nothing there, my ma already ironed his shirt today and told me to hang it in his wardrobe, she's only been winding him up"

“Oh, so I did Duncan, I forgot all about that” my Ma said laughing

Neither Darlene nor I found it funny it wasn’t that often you got a chance to get money from Dunky and we had just missed one.

“I’m not watching all of them ma, me and Susan Dobie are going to the dancing at shuffles tonight, you never asked me to watch them, let Danny watch them for a change” Darlene said having finally got as close to the mirror as she wanted because my Ma was finished with putting on her makeup and pulling her coat on ready to go.

“No” I screamed “No way, I’m, I’m, I’m” I couldn’t think of an excuse quick enough.

“Don’t let Charlie out Danny, keep him in with you, you never know what he’s going to get up to” my Ma said as she cuddled me and kissed my cheek on her way out of the door.

Darlene burst out laughing and said mockingly ”Enjoy being the babysitter Danny, that will be your job forever now, we might start calling you nanny instead of Danny”

Charlie chimed in with “or Fanny”

Paul offered “Danny, the fanny nanny” Wee David joined in with him, they were now holding hands and almost skipping in a circle chanting “Danny is a fanny nanny, Danny is a fanny nanny” over and over again.

So since Paul was the nearest I slapped him, considering he was only six, I could reasonably have expected no response, I was wrong he kicked me straight on the shin bone and bolted, I went down with a cry holding my leg, to the sound of Charlie, Paul and even wee David’s derisive laughter. Just as I thought it couldn’t get any worse, the front door opened and in came big Tony with wee Tony,

“Is it alright if I leave the wee man here with you gorgeous?” Tony asked as he grabbed Darlene round the waist and twirled her around as if they were dancing.

"You can leave him here with Danny if you want, it's no problem to me I'm out of here in ten minutes as soon as Mags and Sally an Susan get here, I'm gone" Darlene said extricating herself from Tony's grasp.

Tony then grabbed me with his arm playfully round my neck, "So you're the man of the house tonight Danny, you don't mind me leaving wee Tony here do you?, he can climb in with Wee David, they will keep each other company, there's ten bob in it for you, how's about it Danny, you know it makes sense wee man"

I decided there and then that this was going to stop, I was thirteen there's no way I was going to spend the next few years looking after my three wee brothers all weekend every weekend, I wouldn't allow it to happen, Darlene was fifteen they could let her look after them and anyway she was a girl it was her job to look after them, but Darlene was no fool she had understood the concept and principals of feminism instinctively.

"Danny, it's time you woke up son, women aren't here to run after men anymore, the platform shoe is on the other boot now" Darlene said when I mumbled out loud that she was a girl and should be babysitting. And what was that supposed to mean anyway, the platform shoe is on the other boot that didn't make sense but before I could righteously accuse her of talking shite, she was gone as was everybody else, including Charlie, see you later fanny nanny Danny he said as he skipped out the front door narrowly avoiding my Da's working boot that I threw at him.

As it turned out it wasn't that bad Paul more or less looked after himself, he played with his wee fort and soldiers for a while and then fell asleep on the floor behind the couch, wee Davey and wee Tony had a bit of a fight, which wee Davey won because as soon as he learned to talk, he learned to say to wee Tony and Donald's oldest son Mark, that he was their uncle and it was ok for him to hit them but definitely not ok for them to hit him, I think they were both about eighteen before they realised that he was bullying them.

Just because the night passed without incident didn't mean I was about to let it become a habit, it was only a couple of months to Christmas and the new year and there was no way I was going to be babysitting all the time while everybody else enjoyed themselves, no chance.

They all started drifting in from the pubs at about half past eleven, my Ma and Da first, and I was extremely pleased to note that it was a smoochy night (for the moment), they paused in the hallway to have a little dance when they heard music coming from the television in the living room, I wasn't yet cynical enough to ask myself how long their smooching would last. Then right behind them came Donnie , as usual without Annie, she rarely made an appearance during the weekend parties, if she did, it was to castigate Donnie and drag him home with screaming allegations of infidelity ringing through his ears.

Ten minutes later Dunky arrived, well he arrived in the street anyway, he could be heard from inside the house singing shang a lang, my Ma lifted her head from my Da's shoulder and asked "Is that our Dunky making all that bloody awful noise" which was a bit of a shame because Dunky thought he was a good singer. I ran to the living room window and shouted back to my Ma, "Aye it is Dunky, he's steaming, he's staggering all over the road and some wee lassie is trying to stop him falling on his bahookey"

My Ma disentangled herself from the waltz my Da was still trying to do and said to him, "go on down and help him up the stair Davie" I couldn't stop myself, I burst out laughing and said "If my Da goes down the stair he might need help to get back up"

"What are you trying to say Danny, I'm serfectly pober" my Da replied "I mean I'm perbectly sofa" he tried again "I'm ok," he finally settled for.

"I'll go and get him Da, you finish your wee dance with my Ma" I said before my Da could realise that I had been cheeky to him and change from smoochy and funny to angry and mean, which could take less than three seconds.

Just as I emerged out of the close Dunky was approaching it and seen me "Danny, wee man, come on meet Bessie, wee man she's a cracking wee bird, Bessie this is Danny my favourite wee brother, well one of my top three favourite wee brothers" his guffaw of laughter at his own joke turned into a retch and a vomit over the hedge into Mrs Wilson's wee bit of garden The girl who looked about to collapse under the strain of holding him up said " My names Jessie son, no Bessie and your favourite big brother here is drunk as a skunk and to think about two hours ago I thought he was a bit of alright, I actually thought he looked a bit like one of the bay city rollers with his feather cut and that, but I canny imagine Eric Faulkner leaning over a hedge vomiting into a garden in Cessnock, och well you live and learn wee man don't you"

She let him go and he flopped halfway over the hedge, and I said to her "Actually Mrs he thought he was one of the Bay City Rollers for a few months, and by the way he is only in the top two of my favourite big brothers"

Just as we both smiled I heard a shrill shout from behind me "Hey you, you tart get away from my man, get your manky hands off him"

I turned to look at the shouty person coming along Cessnock Street from the Govan road end and didn't recognise her, and then I looked the other way towards the Paisley road, in case it was somebody else she was shouting at but couldn'y see anybody. I turned back and looked at Jessie and shrugged my shoulders at her and she shrugged hers at me and said "I haven't got a clue wee man, but tonight just keeps getting better and better" I laughed and said "this is nothing you should come here at the new year" by this time the shouty person had reached us and I finally realise that it must be Elaine, Dunky's fiancé or hatchet face as Darlene preferred to call her.

Without another word Elaine walked straight at Jessie and pushed her full force into the hedge beside Dunky, which bizarrely caused Dunky to roll off the hedge land on his arse and let out a reasonably loud fart at the same time as being sick again all down his front. As much as I wanted to stare at Dunky and fully enjoy his discomfort and eventual embarrassment , as the two women now had a grip of each other's hair I thought I better try and stop them fighting before I could take pleasure in Dunky's predicament.

A shout from above made me look up sharply "Danny, stop them from fighting their making a right show of themselves who are they anyway" my Ma asked as she leaned precariously out of the living room window, and before I could answer Donnie appeared over my Ma's shoulder and shouted "Leave them alone Danny, if they want to fight let them fight, in fact they should strip to the waist and fight like men" My Ma turned round and slapped him and told him to stop being so filthy.

Just at that I heard Darlene's sweet voice shouting "Danny what's the score with they two wee man, are they fighting over you" as she staggered her way along Cessnock street to join the show, then naturally since there's no show without punch, I heard Charlie shouting and laughing, and looking up I spotted him at Searcher's living room window across the street, which I thought was odd since Searcher was away down to Lincoln with his Ma and Da for the weekend, but since Searcher's big sister was standing right beside Charlie trying to hide herself behind the sheet they used as a curtain, I thought I had a good idea why he was up there.

"Gonny stop shouting rubbish Charlie and get your arse down here and help me" I cried

"I'm gonny kill you, you wee tart" from Elaine as she grabbed the other girls hair with both hands and pulled her forward while shaking her from side to side.

My Ma obviously getting her priorities right shouted "Danny stop that swearing, or I'll come down there and belt you one"

Dunky was in a pool of his own vomit and maybe shite as well judging by the smell, two lassie's were battering lumps out of each other in the middle of the entrance to our close, Darlene was steaming and standing pointing and laughing at both Dunky and the two lassies, Charlie was quite obviously up to no good with a fifteen year old lassie across the road, and my Ma thinks the main thing to notice is that I said "Arse"

"Who the hell are you missus and let go of my hair before I really get pissed off and do you in" Jessie responded to Elaine's attack by swinging her arms wildly trying to land a blow on Elaine wherever she could but without much success as Elaine had by now pulled Jessie's head down so that she was completely bent over which made her arm swinging pretty pointless, but Jessie had obviously been in this position before, (Which probably most woman in Glasgow had been as well.) and suddenly surged forward pushing Elaine back against the opposite hedge which allowed Jessie to be almost upright and although Elaine still had a double handed grip on Jessie hair, Jessie was now in a position where she was starting to land blows on Elaine's head and body.

I thought "oh shit" and started shouting "stop it, stop hitting her she's pregnant" This bizarrely seemed to infuriate Elaine, and she started screaming even louder at Jessie "If you're pregnant to my man I mean it I'm gonny stab you, you manky midden"

"Not her you " I shouted at Elaine taking advantage in a slight lull in the fight and getting in between them , and disentangling Elaine's fingernails from Jessie's hair I said with not a little confusion in my voice "It's you that's pregnant Elaine, did you forget or something" she looked at me with a strange expression on her face and said "Aye , seeing that tart trying to molest my Dunky because he's drunk made me forget everything" as she tried to stretch around me and get another grip on Jessie's hair she let out another scream of "beat it you smelly cow before I do something I regret"

Jessie with as much aplomb as she could muster smoothed down her hair and her dress in that order "If you don't mind me telling you something, I think you've already done something you might regret just getting involved with this mob, except you wee man" she said smiling at me through her smeared lipstick. She tottered away on high heels and would have achieved her plan of making a dramatic exit if she hadn't tripped over a hole in the pavement and bounced off the hedge towards the road, only just recovering her balance before shaking her hair and walking away towards the Paisley Road West, as she did Donnie came hurrying out of the close and ran to catch up with her and I could hear him saying, "Aw look at the state she's left you in hen, come on and I'll walk you along to the toll and I'll get you a taxi, it's the least I can do after all the upset you've had"

Darlene looked at Donnie and the departing Jessie and said "she's not falling for that shite is she? Then at Elaine and said "I know you, don't I, you're that lassie from Govan that Dunky got pregnant, you shouldn'y be fighting, not in your conjunction"

"She means condition, but she's right, what possessed you to start a fight, and how can you forget you're expecting " I said turning towards Dunky's sprawled body, wondering how I was going to be able to lift him up without getting covered in vomit. Elaine never answered my question and as I glanced at her she had an odd guilty look on her face.

Before I could try and work out why she looked guilty, Charlie appeared at my side pulling his jumper on over his head and said "I'm not helping you with him, Danny, he's covered in sick, look at the state of him, and hopped over Dunky into the close and stated running up the stairs three at a time.

Naturally I started shouting at him and at my Ma "If nobody's gonny help me then I'm just leaving him there, why should I care, he got himself in this state why has it got anything to do with me, I'm just leaving him here if he chokes on his own vomit, it's not my fault"

Darlene gingerly stepped over the slowly spreading pool of sick at Dunky's feet and said "Stop being so dramatic Danny, and bring him up the stair its getting really freezing out here." She the staggered into the close and climbed the stairs a lot more slowly than Charlie had, she was holding tight to the banister with both hands and going up the stairs sideways, when one of her stiletto's fell off she cried stuff it and kicked her other one off, and slurred to me "Danny, bring they shoe's up the stair when you're finished pissing about with Dunky"

I stood there and screamed at the top of my voice "I'm not bringing him up the stair myself, he's too heavy and he's covered in sick"

"Do you want a hand wee man, you look like you're having a bit of bother" this came from a big guy who was getting out of a sports car which had just pulled up a couple of closes down from Searchers close, the car looked like something out of James Bond and the guy himself must have been at least six feet three, which made him a veritable giant in Glasgow.

The sound of his voice made Darlene pause in her attempts to drag herself upstairs and she turned and looked, clearly noticing him and his car at the same time and she said "Oh look Danny a shite in whining armour" and promptly fell down the few stairs she had managed to climb so far.

The big guy ran to her and said come on hen I think we better get you up the stairs to your bed, Darlene not missing a chance to show her true ladylike qualities said "Ok but you will need to sneak in past my Ma and Da" The big guy just laughed and lifted her bodily off the floor and into her arms.

Darlene said "I think I can walk ok" and as he started to set her down she hurriedly added "I think I can walk, but that doesn'y mean I want to" and smiled what I can only presume she thought was a seductive smile at him, it would probably have worked better if there wasn't a bit of green stuff on her teeth.

"What about him" I pointed at Dunky and shouted at the guy's back as he climbed the stairs with Darlene in his arms like something out of Gone with the wind.

“Hold on to your knickers wee man I’ll be down in a minute” I was about to bristle at him calling me wee man and then realised what height he was and accepted my lot.

He took about half an hour to come down the stairs, it turns out his name was John Lawson and he knew Charlie because he worked in a garage in Brand Street which Charlie went into every day collecting ginger bottles. When between us we managed to get Dunky up the stairs and into the bedroom, not actually into the bed but sprawled near it, but at least we managed to strip his sick encrusted jumper off him, I got told to make tea for John and we sat at the kitchen table and found out a little bit more about him. When I say we, I mean My Ma, Charlie, Darlene and Me, because as the drama had been unfolding downstairs My Da had fallen asleep on the couch and nobody was willing to move him, because when you woke my Da out of a drunken sleep he came out swinging punches, my Ma told me one day many years later that she thought he was like that because somebody tried to interfere with him sexually when he was in the army doing his national service, but I think she was just being vindictive by that point.

John told us the car actually belonged to the garage but he was allowed to take it home until a buyer could be found for it, he told Charlie that he would come and pick him and me up the next morning and take us for a run to loch Lomond if we fancied it, and he would even take the top down on the car if it wasn’t raining. Naturally since we didn’t know him from Adam Darlene offered to come along to look after us, aye right.

Charlie and I were up at seven o’clock sitting by the living room window looking out for the red sports car, we waited for a while in fact we waited nearly two hours before Darlene decided to fight her hangover by actually getting out of bed, albeit she looked like she had been dragged through a hedge backwards she spotted us at the window and said “What are you two wee retards sitting at the window for John said he wouldn’y be here until about eleven o’clock, and anyway, I’ve told my Ma that we don’t even know this guy, really, so it’s best if I just go out with him to loch Lemon today and if he turns out to be okay then you two can go with him another time"

Charlie looked at me and then at her and then back to me, "Did you understand a single word that she said there Danny, it sounded to me like she said, listen Charlie and Danny I know you fancy a wee trip in a sports car out to Loch Lomond today, but I'm gonny stop you from doing that, but while I'm away doing that feel free to open up all the drawers in my dressing table and shite in them please"

I burst out laughing and said "you were nearly right Charlie she also added, if you canny manage to shit in all of the drawers feel free to pish in some of them, and that goes for my wardrobe as well."

Darlene, even in her semi comatose state screamed "Ma" and ran out of the living room and into my Ma & Da's bedroom squealing at the top of her lungs "They're gonny shite in my clothes" she retreated out of the bedroom just as quick when my Da threw one of his working boots at her. Which missed her head by inches and left a nice wee two inch hole in the wall where the steel toe cap had hit it, I think it would probably have left the same hole in her head if it had hit her but maybe not, if she thought that we weren't going for a run today then her head was obviously thicker than the wall.

My Ma came in the living room about ten minutes later having obviously been told by my Da to sort us out, "What have I told you about running about screaming in the morning, especially a bloody Sunday morning, your Da's still in bed reading the papers and you're running about screaming like a banshee, that will be him up to high doh all day now because of you, and anyway you're not going anywhere with that boy from last night by yourself, either take they two with you or forget it"

Just as Darlene was straining to comprehend what my Ma was telling her (I know she was straining by the look on her face) somebody in the street started whistling really loud. This brought my Da out of his bed like a bear that had been forced out from its cave.

“Who the fuck is that whistling, it’s Sunday bloody morning can I not get reading the paper in peace, as if you squealing like a burst boiler isn’t enough” he shouted at Darlene loud enough to be heard in Govan.

Charlie being Charlie answered him “Da, it’s that guy John Dawson, Darlene’s new boyfriend that’s whistling up for her”

I don’t know how he managed it but my Da got even angrier “Whistling on her? fucking whistling on her? What the fuck is she? a fucking wee dog or something” he screamed as he moved towards the window, I managed to stop Charlie from answering my Da’s rhetorical question by pulling him away from the window thereby giving my Da space to throw the window up so hard it rattled in its frame to such an extent that I’ve got no idea why it didny smash into a thousand bits.

“He was almost on the window ledge when he shouted at John Dawson “Who the fuck do you think you’re whistling on you lanky big streak of pish, that’s my fucking daughter no some wee fucking mongrel”

“All right Jimmy keep your hair on I was only whistling to let her know I was waiting on her, calm down for fuck sake” was John Dawson’s ill considered reply.

That was it, I sat there absolutely believing that my Da’s head might actually explode he went pure red and I would swear on a bible I saw steam coming out of his ears, he looked exactly like somebody in the Beano being mad.

He actually ran out of the living room, which was a rare a sight as seeing Darlene reading a book, no actually scratch that I had actually seen my Da run once before, whereas I had never actually seen Darlene reading anything, even if she looked at a comic like Jackie or something it was clear she was only looking at the pictures, anyway my Da ran out of the living room and straight out the front door I bolted after him and he ran down the stairs four at a time, he was absolutely raging, I had never seen him this angry and believe me I had seen him angry before, the last time had been when his Ma, my Granny Marshall (she remarried after my Da's Da died) had been visiting us and she was sitting at the window looking down into Cessnock street and turned to my Ma and said "Will you look at them two wee rascals Maggie, they're stealing things off the back at that alpine lorry every time the driver goes to do a delivery, you wonder how people bring their weans up these days" The two wee rascals were Charlie and me, my Da went ballistic, to be fair I think my Ma goaded him into being as mad as he was, just because my granny was there.

But anyway, this time he was even madder, he flew down the stairs and went straight at John Dawson, who promptly jumped over Mrs Wilson's hedge and landed in her front garden, without any effort at all, I did say he was a big guy. My Da turned back and went through the gate into Mrs Wilson's garden and John leapt over the hedge again onto the street, My Da tried another two or three times to get near him, he even tried to unsuccessfully leap the hedge as John had done, ending up once or twice on his back either in or out of the hedge, but each time he got anywhere near, John just nipped over the hedge again as if it wasn't there , it was actually quite funny, but no way was anybody laughing. My Da stood in the garden leaning on the gate puffing and panting and struggling to speak "Danny, pick up that big stick there and break this skinny bastards legs so I can catch him"

I looked at the big stick he was pointing at, it was a rotten old branch and then at looked at John Dawson and then looked back at my Da and said "I'm going to get Dunky" and ran into the close, as I reached the first flight of stairs I heard John Dawson shout up to Darlene "I've not got all day hen, if you fancy a wee run I'll be round in Brand street till about twelve o'clock" and then he gave a final hop over the fence and he was into his car and away before my Da could even straighten up.

"Over my dead fucking body" my Da shouted at him as he sped away tires squealing. Darlene wasn't the brightest bulb on the Christmas tree but she knew how to play my Da, "Aye that's right, piss off you big lanky" she shouted when John was clearly out of earshot. She immediately then sprinted to her room patently anxious to get spruced up for her run out to loch lemon. It turns out that it mattered John Dawson was to become her first husband a year or so later.

Charlie took out his frustration at not going to Loch Lomond in the sports car by pulling my hair and declaring it "was all my stupid fault" I retaliated by jumping on top of him and rolling about the hall floor with both of us punching and kicking each other like a rolling ball of arms and legs, when my Da eventually managed to huff and puff his way up the stairs, he took one look at us and said "For fuck sake Maggie will you come and sort these two out, what is it with this family, have they got nothing better to do than fight?" My old man sometimes struggled with irony.

Chapter ten (1975-1976)

Dunky's wedding and other mistakes.

Nineteen seventy five started with a big bust up, which Involved Elaine Murray, Dunky's fiancé, this was becoming a bit of a pattern with her, she seemed to be able to start a fight in an empty room, my Ma reckoned it was because she was pregnant, some women apparently become a bit aggressive when they're pregnant, Dorothy and Darlene both reckoned it was down to Elaine being a wee trouble making cow.

Another hogmanay another rammy, 1974 was on its way out with a whimper as usual we were all gathered in my Ma's house, my Ma and Dorothy were in the kitchen rolling out great big sheets of puff pastry for the steak pies for later on, it was getting near feeding the five thousand with all the new weans that were being dropped on a regular basis by Annie and Dorothy and now Elaine was joining in as well.

Everybody was there Annie had her three weans with her, they always seemed to be attached to her with bits of string whenever she stood up to go somewhere the three of them followed her, although wee Mark was beginning to break that habit as he now formed a trio of terror with wee David and wee Tony, whenever anything was broken, which was usually caused by them singing their new anthem "Kung Fu Fighting" and throwing themselves bodily at each other, or when biscuits or sweets went astray, any question of who did what was met by all three of them pointing at each other and saying "It was him"

"Ma, it's nearly ten o'clock and Danny won't let me in the bathroom to get ready, it's nearly the bells gonny tell him Ma, he's getting on my wick" Darlene punctuated her screaming with heavy pounding on the bathroom door.

"I'm having a bath ya eejit, I'll be out in five minutes now beat it and pick out whatever mask you're wearing tonight to hide your ugliness Darlene" was my witty (in my opinion) retort.

"Ma, gonny tell him please, look at the time" this was elevated to a screech that could have been heard in outer Mongolia, but only by dogs"

"I'm out, I'm out calm down, you've still got two hours to hide your plooks , do you want me to and find some cement" I asked again giggling at my own wonderful talent for humour.

"Find this fanny Danny" Darlene said and punched me straight on the nose, I was confused because what she said was meaningless, what did "find this" mean, if she meant find her fist, it was almost up my nose, how hard would it be to find, it was this momentary confusion that stopped me responding in kind immediately. But it was only a couple of seconds before I grabbed her by the hair and started to swing punches, this action coincided with two things, my Da walking out of the living room and the towel which was wrapped round my waist dislodging itself and slipping down my legs and tangling itself round my ankles causing me to fall to the floor whilst still holding Darlene's hair in one hand and lashing out with the other at her face.

My Da pulled me up from the floor by my arm, almost wrenching it out of its socket, "Stop hitting your sister, what kind of man are you" he shouted in my face "Do you think you're a big man, eh? Hitting a woman doesn't make you a big man" he continued to shout as he dragged me away from Darlene towards my room. There was blood gushing from my nose where Darlene had connected with her haymaker, I was trying desperately to grab the towel from the floor to at least cover my modesty and to cap it all Charlie came in through the front door, with Elaine, Dunky's fiancé right behind him.

As Darlene tried with all her might to reach round my Da and inflict more damage on my burst nose and scratched face, Charlie grabbed her and said "Who lit the fuse on your Tampax" this actually made me stop struggling with my Da and laugh, My Da, apparently speechless, loosened his grip on me slightly enough that I stretched out and finally got hold of the towel and pulled enough of it in front of me to hide my embarrassment , I was trying to use the towel to both cover myself and wipe at the blood streaming from my nose, it wasn't that big a towel.

Charlie had Darlene in a held against a wall and said, you better beat it Danny, if a let her go she might kill you" he then turned to Darlene and said, "and what have I told you, don't fight with ugly people they have got nothing to lose" I wriggled out of my Da's loose grip and bolted into my Bedroom. My Da banged on my door just as I slammed it and shouted the last thing I wanted to hear "And you can stay in there all night, there's no bells for you tonight boy"

I wanted to come tearing out of the room and scream at him, about how unfair that was, about how Darlene had started it all, about how come I always got the blame, about how everybody picked on me, and about how everybody hated me and they could all go to hell" but I didn't because even though I was nearly fifteen and probably believed all those things to be fundamental truths I also knew my Da and knew that if I wanted to remain amongst the living, even without participation in "the bells", them it was time to shut up, this was still nineteen seventy four, teenage strops hadn't been invented yet, well not for boys anyway.

The minutes ticked by exceedingly slowly, I tried three times to ignore My Da's order to stay in my room and just brazenly came out of the room into the kitchen, the first time I did was to find Darlene standing at a mirror in the kitchen, trying in vain to cover up the small black eye which was rapidly forming, when she spotted me she again lost her temper for some unknown reason. "Da, Da" she shouted "There's Danny out of his room, he's just ignoring you Da, Da can you hear me" with a big grin on her face. Rather than facing the music I went back to my room slowly as if the prospect if my Da shouting at me didn't frighten the proverbial out of me.

The second time I came out of the room was to answer a knock at the front door at about half past eleven, because my bedroom is actually the nearest room to the front door, I imagined me answering the front door would be an acceptable reason for me leaving my room, not so. As soon as I left the room and before I had even reached the front door, there was a chorus from Darlene, Charlie and even wee Mark David and Tony "Da, (Granda) Danny's out of his room again"

I didn't actually bother trying to escape again, the third time I left the room which was a bit later wasn't my decision, I just stayed in my room through the bells, almost immediately after the bells the four youngest children were all put into my room in various stages of sleep with instructions to me to put them into bed, I'm not sure how I was supposed to do that, there was a single bed and a set of bunk beds in my room I was on the single bed, both of the bunk beds were covered in a virtual mountain of coats, which had been thrown in by the multitude of visitors who frequent our house at "the bells". As they had all trooped in to deposit their coats I had varying comments all night, every time one of them came in.

"Aw, are you no well son, why are you in your bed already, aw that's a shame so it is" by Mrs Wilson who lived in the bottom flat of the close.

"Why are you in here wee man, all the drink and grub is in the living room, do you want me to sneak you in a sausage roll and a wee half" from one of Dorothy's old boyfriends.

"Is there somebody under the covers with you there wee man, and if there isn't do you want me to send one of Darlene's pals ben" From Tony, Dorothy's husband.

"Oh sorry wee man, I didn't realise you were in bed, have you had too much to drink already, do you need a wee basin to be sick in" From one of Donald's workmates.

"Och you poor soul what have you done to be sent in here, and look at that face och what a bloody liberty, locking you in here at the bells, a damn shame" from one of my Ma's drunken pals from the Camden bar, she also almost suffocated me pulling me into her ample bosom to console me, I thought she was never going to let me go.

I took to diving under the single bed every time I heard anybody coming in the front door, it was easier that way because as the night went on, the visitors became more and more drunk and on one occasion very amorous, it was again a drunken women friend of my Ma's (not the same one with the ample bosom) this one came into the room with a man basically entwined with her to such an extent it would have been near impossible to get a cigarette paper between them, their passion seen them collapse on to the bottom of my bed all ready to get even more passionate and I think it was only my squeal of "For fuck sake watch my legs" that made them keep their clothes on, as they left with a hurried oops sorry wee man, I could swear the guy involved was Dorothy's old boyfriend and not the husband of the women involved, but I didn't know them that well so maybe I got it wrong, but she certainly looked very flustered as they escaped back into the hall.

The third time I finally escaped was because of all the fighting that was going on in the hall outside my bedroom door. It was nearly five o'clock in the morning Annie was in my room settling her youngest, Duncan down after his latest feed when we heard a commotion in the hall, I jumped out of my bed and opened my bedroom door, it was bedlam. Since I didn't see the start of all this I can only tell you what I heard the next day after the event.

Darlene told me more or less that most of what happened had actually probably been my fault, which in hindsight was fair enough, after all I wasn't there, I was asleep or at the very least imprisoned in my bedroom with four smelly weans and a mountain of coats, and on past performance whenever I'm not there whatever happened was my fault, her reasoning for it being my fault was interesting though. You see I had delayed her getting ready, and forced her to punch me in the face, which had put everybody in a bad mood, which only got worse as the night wore on due to everybody that came in saying to my Da, you should let the wee man out of the bedroom its "the bells" after all, because this made the mood worse, that was the reason she eventually punched Elaine in the face. Do you get it? Darlene punched me in the face for nothing, causing her to be in such a bad mood that she had to punch Dunky's pregnant and drunk fiancé in the face. See definitely my fault, guilty as charged.

What actually happened was that apparently Darlene had been dancing with Tony and, a drunken Tony being a drunken Tony had been going slightly over the top and twice swung her around his waist as if jiving, on both occasions Darlene's feet had either narrowly missed or just caught Elaine's stomach who both times let out a scream and a foul mouthed reminder that she was pregnant and why couldn't Darlene be more effing careful. Except she didn't say effing.

Darlene then pirouetted out of Tony's grasp and into the arms of her big brother Dunky whereupon she gave him a big slobbery kiss and declared her love for him, this riled Elaine even more and she hissed at Darlene "Hey you get of my man you wee tart, stop kissing him like that"

Darlene looked perplexed, which to be fair Darlene often did, but although she struggled to form a response to Elaine she eventually spluttered " What are you talking about, he's my big brother I'll kiss him if I want and no wee skinny runt from Govan is going to stop me" Elaine then pushed Darlene away from Dunky and said "This wee skinny runt from Govan can stop you dead easy, what is it with you McCallister women, you're like bitches on heat you even slabber all over your own brothers it's really creepy how close you'se all are"

That was the point at which Elaine, three months pregnant Elaine, got the same treatment I had, a punch straight on the bridge of her nose, she bled just as profusely as I had, but with the advantage of not being naked. Elaine didn't take being punched in the face any better than me and reacted in a remarkably similar manner by grabbing Darlene by the hair and throwing punches, maybe it's a Glasgow reaction to being punched on the nose, who knows.

As they struggled with each other the melee made its way out of the living room and into the hall, which is when I opened my bedroom door and witnessed the rest of it myself. Elaine and Darlene were still going at it full tilt when my Ma came out of the toilet and seen them, she immediately went across and joined the throng who were trying to separate them and keep them apart, my Ma's voice carried total authority in my house so when she raised it you listened, she shouted "Right that's enough both of you Darlene stop it and let go of Elaine's hair, Elaine let Darlene go right now, you'se two aren't weans pack it in" Darlene relaxed her hold, which allowed Elaine to turn round and slap my Ma, on her left cheek.

Total stunned silence, you could have heard a pin drop, in fact you could have heard an eyelash drop. She slapped My Ma, right in the face, my ma, on her face, she slapped her. It was probably only seconds but it seemed like ages that everybody just stood there aghast, then Dorothy reacted first and grabbed Elaine by the throat and pushed her against the wall beside the front door, until Elaine's feet actually left the floor, bear in mind Dorothy is only four foot ten.

"Dunky, get this thing out of here take her home, or take her and dump her in the street like a mangy old dog, I don't care, just get rid of her, because if you don't I'm going to strangle the life out of her pregnant or not" Dorothy almost whispered this threat all the while looking straight at Elaine whilst talking at Dunky.

Dunky roughly grabbed Elaine and said "Out, move it" I ran into my bedroom and threw Elaine's coat to Dunky before he closed the front door behind them, Darlene looked venomously at me and all I could say was "It's freezing out there"

Party over, you would think, not in our house, the women screeched for a few minutes, the men laughed as the tension released and Darlene said "Da, Danny's out of his room" My Da said to his drunken credit, "What, what are you talking about Darlene, Danny come on into the living room and tell Tony about you nearly beating me at chess the other night"

"The Bells" stopped metaphorically ringing just before noon when even the hardiest of drinkers had to admit defeat to the body's demands for sleep or more accurately in some cases, self induced coma. My Ma emerged at about four o'clock with the phrase which was never far from her lips "Danny, tea" the women of the family sat at the kitchen table, as usual, discussing the ins and outs of the night before, while I made copious amounts of tea and poured just as many glasses or even mugs of irn bru, although Darlene was equally as happy drinking from the bottle rather than a tumbler or mug. The consensus was that Elaine had quite deliberately slapped my Ma, the only person dissenting from that view was my Ma herself.

“It was an accident, she was fighting with Darlene and when I got in between them her hand hit my face by accident” she said quietly.

“No it wisnae Ma, I had let the stupid cow go and she actually turned round and thumped you that wisnae an accident, and if it was, just wait and see the accident I’m gonny give her after she has that wean” Darlene responded without lifting her head from the kitchen table where it appeared to be glued down.

“She’s right Maggie” Annie said “I was sober as a judge, and there was no way that was an accident, she meant to it absolutely sure, she is a nasty wee piece of work that one”

Dorothy just looked at my Ma and shook her head (listen to them Ma, they’re right.

“That lassie is gonny be married to Dunky in February, and that means she becomes part of the family, my family, that means it was an accident, and that’s final, Darlene I want you to go down to her ma’s house and apologise to Elaine and let her know there are no hard feelings it was only a drunken argument” My Ma said to the top of Darlene’s head.

Darlene mumbled “No”

“Darlene sit up and look at me when I’m talking to you, go tonight and see that lassie and tell her you’re sorry, I’m not asking you I’m telling you, and I’m not telling you again” my Ma said with a bit more emphasis.

“Och Ma for f.., god’s sake, it was her that started it” Darlene began but as she raised her head and saw my Ma’s face she changed tack slightly and let her head slump down on to the table again before saying “Right ok right I will then, I’ll go and tell her I’m sorry she’s a foul mouthed ugly skinny wee ratbag” my ma only got the first syllable out “Dar” before Darlene capitulated and again without raising her head said “Ok ok ok, I’ll apologise but I canny vouch for my temper if she starts again”

“Dorothy will you give her a walk down to Govan and make sure you she disnae start anything” my Ma asked Dot. But before Dot could answer Dunky popped his head round the door and said, “Ma, Elaine’s down in the close she wants to come up and apologise, but she disnae want Dot or Darlene to start throwing punches at her again”

“Tell her to come up the stair Duncan, nobody will tough her” my Ma said, both Darlene and Dorothy scowled and growled but said nothing.

Elaine looked a bit sheepish as she came into the kitchen but not completely there was still a bit of fire in her apology, “Mrs McCallister I’m sorry about last night I swear on my weans life, I didnae mean to hit you it was a total accident, I was just trying to defend myself from her” she said with a disparaging tone on the word “her”, and pointed at Darlene.

“Don’t do that hen, don’t swear on your weans life that’s a terrible thing to say, I already know it was an accident, I’ve just finished saying that, Danny get Elaine a cup of tea son”

“What do you take in your tea Elaine” I asked trying to inject some friendliness in my voice.

“Rat poison” Darlene interjected.

Dunky grabbed Darlene but before he could remonstrate with her My Ma said “Darlene do you know something hen, I’m getting really fed up with you lashing out at everybody and then blaming them for what you started you did the same to Danny last night, so beat it, get your drunken head off the table and get to your bed, Dunky let her go, go on Darlene move get out of my sight, Danny pour Elaine’s tea, come on sit down hen, we need to start talking about the wedding anyway, move Darlene that’s your last warning”

As Darlene huffily got to her feet and stormed towards the kitchen door I said “I would make you a cup Darlene but I’m out of rat poison” not very funny I know, but I was fourteen it seemed funny to me at the time.

Things settled down over the next few weeks the problems that Darlene and Dot had with Elaine were partly solved by them all doing their best not to be in the same room, there was still a fair amount of threats and bluster coming from Darlene whenever Elaine's name was mentioned, Dot kept her opinion mostly to herself although I did over hear her ask my Ma if it was wise for Dunky to get married to Elaine if it was going to be like this all the time, in fact she said it seemed as if Dunky wasn't that happy about the wedding. My Ma said, "Well if Dunky had managed to do his thinking whilst standing up instead of when he was lying down, he wouldn't be in this position, so he's had the fun and now he has to pay for it, and if he's not happy then that's just tough "

Whatever the surrounding circumstance, all of the women were still up for a wedding, this one might not have the usual amount of underlying joy and excitement but it was still an excuse for a new outfit, or in Darlene's case three or four new outfits to choose from, although to be fair only one of them was bought the others were borrowed.

She was in the middle of her very own fashion parade walking up and down the hallway as Annie and my Ma watched her and listened to her commentary on each outfit, she had just started her commentary on what looked to me like a flowery orange boiler suit when Charlie and I arrived home from having been playing football in the park, to say were a bit mucky is like saying Antarctica is a bit cold, we were basically layered in mud.

"What is that you've got on, Darlene is it a fancy dress party tonight"" Charlie said laughing semi hysterically.

Darlene haughtily responded "Actually this is a Mary Quant inspired, sepia tinged orange one piece bell bottomed leisure suit, with puffed shoulders and a prominent chrysanthemum print. Which I bought out of Kirkwood's today and it cost a fortune if you must know"

I think Charlie might actually have wet himself, he was laughing so hard, if he hadn't wet himself, he was probably about to. He stood there with his legs crossed and going ever redder in the face, trying to splutter something or other. Eventually he managed to get his hysteria under control and said "Aw Darlene, I know you think it looks trendy but honest to god you look as if you have had a fight with a big pair of curtains and you lost"

I had to agree with him she did look ridiculous it was the nearest thing I had ever seen to a clown suit, if she wore a pair of my Da's working boots and painted her nose red she would have been a dead ringer for Bozo the clown, so being me, I told her that.

"You'se two are ignorant cheeky wee bastard's and you'se widnae know a single thing about fashion anyway, just imagine me listening to anything you'se had to say about clothes, look at you'se, you'se are horrible manky wee tramps. I don't even know what colour you really are because I've never actually seen you when your clean, for all I know you could be a couple of wee packies. Ma gonny tell them to stop being rotten to me they're a couple of wee bast.."

"Darlene stop swearing and don't rise to them, I think you look really glamorous , one of the bond girls had a leisure suit just like that on in that film last year, what was it called again" Annie offered her opinion.

Darlene answered "The man with the golden finger, and it was that foreign lassie Brick Eckling that was in it and you're right she did have an outfit like this on, so you'se two can piss off."

Before we could either correct her about the name of the film or piss off as instructed , Dorothy came out of Darlene's bedroom with a similar suit on except it was lime green and asked Darlene and Annie "Does my arse look big in this ".

I answered with my mouth before my brain knew what it was doing (as usual) "It's not the suit that makes your arse look big, it's your big fat arse that makes your arse look big" Dot should probably have played baseball or cricket or something because whenever she threw anything at me, it always hit me right on the head, this time it was one of her shoes which she had been holding, I suppose I'm actually quite lucky that it wasn't the stiletto heel end which could have just stuck in my forehead,

I immediately decided that being a fashion critic was too painful and headed for the bathroom but before I could get there my Ma screamed at me "Where do you think you're going with that mud all over you, get out on the stair landing and strip all of they mucky clothes off, yours not stopping all the bath up with that mud, you as well Charlie, stripped"

It was then a race to see who could get out of the muddy clothes first and into the bath. Charlie won, but only because he took his jumper off and threw it right over my face so by the time I got that off he had stripped down to his pants and bolted right into the bathroom. Brilliant, I had to stand out on the landing stripped to my pants waiting for him to come out of the bath, remember it was Glasgow in the middle of February, it wisnae warm. To make it worse, before I could stop her Darlene shut the door in my face and said "Stay out there till you freeze you wee shite" I could hear them all laughing even my Ma.

It was more than half an hour before wee Paul came and let me in. I had been shouting through the letter box for the first ten minutes but gave up and just sat on the stairs with the muddy shirts round my shoulders.

"What are you doing out there Danny Fanny, are you no freezing" Wee Paul said and jumped out of the way of the kick I aimed at him.

"Is Charlie out of that bath yet?" I asked my Ma as she walked across the hall heading for the kitchen.

When she indicated that he was I approached the bathroom door and found it to be locked from the inside. For the past week or so Charlie had been playing the same trick over and over again. The lock in the inside of the bathroom door was a wee brass snib, if you put a bit of string round that snib you could lock it from the outside and cause a queue of McCallisters to form a line waiting to get in to the toilet, I knew of his trick and didn't let on to anybody else because it was actually quite funny seeing Darlene standing squirming outside the toilet door, at least three times this week she had went next door and used our neighbours toilet. It was also reasonably funny to see wee Paul trying to rent out his old po for five pence a pee and ten pence for a jobby.

Suffice to say it was annoying everybody, so naturally I assumed this to be the situation and I let out an angry yell "Charlie you wee shit you are getting on my nerves" and kicked the door open, to reveal my Da sitting on the toilet reading his Daily Express newspaper. I scarpered thinking that I was off my mark so fast that he hadn't seen me, I got seven steps before he bellowed for me to stand still. So that's exactly what I did, I stood still. Over the next couple of days as I started to get some feeling back in my arse, I more or less decided that my life was going to follow this route forever, Charlie screws up, Danny pays the penalty, how much is the fare to Australia?, one way.

<u>The day of the wedding.</u>

This wedding seemed to have been a lot more low key than Donald and Annie's or Dorothy and Tony's, maybe it was because there's was a double wedding that there seemed to be a lot more excitement in the weeks leading up to it, or maybe it was just that all four of them and everybody else were happy for their weddings to be taking place.

"What's up with your face, it's your wedding day, try smiling, it's no sore once you get used to it" Donald was saying to Dunky as I woke up, they had both stayed the night before due to the stag night being in the Camden and it was easier for Donald to come here rather than go home.

I asked what time it was, which was apparently an excuse for Donnie to leap on top of me and say "It's time you were up Danny the fanny and making your big brother's breakfast, the condemned man is entitled to a last meal after all"

"Why has Annie had you condemned, is it because you look like a slum" I retorted doing my best to push him off me, with little success.

Charlie reached down from the top bunk and grabbed one of Donald's ears and said "Maybe you should leave my brother alone and go and get your woman to make your breakfast or are you too feart"

Ordinarily you would presume that a thirteen year old would have more respect or at least more fear of his twenty five year old sibling, not so with Charlie.

Donald stood up on the side of the bottom bunk and started pummelling Charlie through the blankets that he had retreated under after coming to my rescue. I thought at first that Donald was playing with Charlie as he had been with me, but I quickly realised that the punches he was aiming at Charlie through the blankets carried some weight behind them.

I kicked at Donald's legs and then escaped from the bottom bunk and dragged Donald down by getting a grip of his belt and pulling. "What's the matter with you, stop punching him he was only having a laugh" I shouted as I struggled to hold Donald back from his assault on Charlie.

Dunky pushed past me without joining in at all, I would normally expect Dunky to jump in to any fight, real or otherwise on Donnie's side, that's the way it normally worked but he just pushed past with no interest at all in our childish squabbles.

"What's up with him, have the Bay City Rollers knocked back his application" Charlie asked sarcastically.

"No, the price of Hai Karate has just went up" I responded in kind.

"Leave him alone both of you, he's just nervous" Donnie said.

“It’s his wedding day Donnie, is he no supposed to be happy, you and Tony weren’t like this, you’se two were half drunk and having a laugh” I asked.

“Aye but they too are a lot more stupid than Dunky” Charlie said and ducked back under his blankets before Donnie had a chance to whack him again, but Donnie didn’t even try he just followed Dunky out of the room looking equally as worried.

Later on, I was on tea making duty (imagine that) when I heard the front door opening and a voice shouting “It’s only me, stand by your beds and cover up your rude bits” It was Annie and she had the three kids in tow as usual and her wee sister Shirley Anne the hairdresser who did all of the lassies hairdo’s at Dot’s wedding.

“Oh good boy Danny put me out a cup milk and two sugars and I’ll give that hair of yours a wee trim for nothing or do you fancy a curly perm?” Shirley Anne said cackling away at her own joke.

“I’ll make you a cup but you don’t need to bother with the hairdo thanks very much” I answered sarcastically, you might or might not remember but Shirley Anne has got a skelly eye and I have no idea why anybody would trust her with a pair of scissors in her hand.

“Put me out a cup as well Danny my wee darling” Annie said grabbing me and cuddling me as she invariably did.

“Here Annie he’s getting a bit big for all that cuddling now, mind you don’t get him overexcited” Shirley Anne cackled again before continuing “What age are you now Danny” she answered her own question before I could say anything “nearly fifteen, aren’t you, you’re not a bad looking boy a bit wee but not too wee, give me a shout when you’re sixteen I’ll see what I can do about breaking you in, or maybe even see how drunk I get the day and chance your arm wee man” She thought this was so funny she virtually had to double over to properly cackle.

Annie tried to sound furious with her but the smile on her face told a different story. “You leave him alone you wee tart, you’re an old woman compared to him (She was twenty two), any way Danny prefers his books to women, don’t you Danny”

My mouth hung open. I stammered and stuttered something about the kettle boiling and scurried in to the kitchen, to the sound of raucous laughter behind me.

I stood at the kitchen sink rinsing out some cups with cold water, had I run the water over my face first it would have come to the boil in seconds “Are you gonny try and ride her if you get drunk” Charlie whispered to me as he silently appeared behind me.

“Fuck off” I said “what would you know about riding anyway” I responded still bright crimson.

“A lot more than you” Charlie said laughing “For instance I know doing it is a lot better than reading about it”

“Fuck off” I said “Doing it with your right hand yourself disnae count”

“No, no, that’s just yourself you’re thinking about I’m talking about doing it with Betty, Searchers big sister” Charlie said with a big beaming grin on his face, which actually had me thinking he might be telling the truth, unbelievable as it was.

“Fuck off” I said “When”

“A few weeks ago, remember the night Darlene and Elaine were kicking the shit out of each other and I shouted down from Searcher’s window, that night” he said, exhibiting a look on his face that told me he was probably being honest for once, his pride in this was unmistakable.

“Fuck off” I said “She’s nearly seventeen, you’re only thirteen, what is she a cradle snatcher”

“Sounds like you’re a wee bit jealous there Danny boy, do you want me to tell you how it’s done” he said almost unable to contain his glee, and grabbed me thrusting his pelvis forward as he did.

“Fuck off” I said and pushed him away “I did it a long time before you even knew what it was and it wisnae with sweaty Betty either” sounding, even to myself, less than totally convincing.

“No you didnae, you big fat liar” Charlie laughed at my poor attempt at one-upmanship.

“Fuck off” I said “aye I did, but as if I would tell you anything about it you wee pervert, just because I don’t take an advert out in the paper disnae mean it didny happen” I was starting to actually convince myself.

“Who was it then, was it some auld prossie down the docks” Charlie said remaining completely unconvinced by my assertions, and clearly thoroughly enjoying my discomfort.

“Fuck off” I said, frantically trying to think of a name “It was Sally Malcolm, Darlene’s pal, who’s actually nineteen now, nearly twenty”

“No you didnae” came both from Charlie stood beside and Darlene stood behind me. Charlie looked absolutely delighted, Darlene looked crazy. “Tell me that was a lie Danny, because if you really did do it with Sally, then I’m gonny batter you and then I’m gonny batter her ten times worse” she said grabbing me by the shirt and getting right up in my face.

“Fuck off, leave me alone” I said and scrambled away from her half ripping my shirt in the process and fled from the kitchen.

“Fuck off” I said to myself as I sat on the edge of my bed crying, “why did you go and say that”

Darlene wasn’t for letting it go, she stormed into the room and demanded” Don’t mess about Danny tell me right now if it’s true, did Sally Malcolm mollycoddle you, I mean molest you”

Even through my tears I had to giggle, “No Darlene she didnae, mollycoddle or molest me, I was just saying that to annoy that wee lying bastard ben there”

Darlene nodded and tried to put what she considered a wise and big sisterly tone in her voice and a similar look on her face when she suggested, “if you want to talk about anything like that, I mean about lassies and how they’re different from boys and that, you can ask me I don’t mind, I know weans like you get curious sometimes about thingwy, you know”

“No, Darlene I don’t want to ask you any questions about the physical differences between the male and female reproductive systems, or the different psychological ways that both sexes approach procreation, where the female of the species have a much higher propensity to engage emotionally in the process whereas the male of the species almost exclusively sees it has a seed scattering exercise and will feign emotional attachment in order to propagate that seed.” I said grinning.

Her mouth hung open for a second or two and she replied “You can be a right wee prick sometimes, I’m trying to be a big sister and help you through pubensity and you are just making words up and talking shite and thinking I’m daft, I’m no daft, it’s you that’s daft if you shagged Sally Malcolm, you will probably get VB”

She stood up and stormed back out of the room, I jumped up and ran into the hall behind her and shouted triumphantly “It’s VD, ya eejit”

As the word eejit left my mouth my Ma walked out of the living room and stared at me “What’s VD Danny?” she said.

I was struggling to breathe how much worse was I going to make this with my stupid unstoppable mouth. Annie and Shirley Anne then walked out of the kitchen and said in harmony, “VD, who’s got VD?” This was becoming a three ringed circus and I was obviously the head clown. So I did what anybody with any sense would do and screamed “Leave me alone, all of you get aff my back, you'se are always picking on me" and slammed my bedroom door shut behind me.

"For god's sake who stole his dummy?" Annie asked.

"Probably Pubensity" Darlene offered as her explanation "He's at that age"

"What the hell is pubensity Darlene do you mean puberty, well he's definitely through puberty Darlene, I should know I wash his sheets" My ma said and they all laughed as if it was the funniest thing they had ever heard.

I didn't think that the day could get any worse but it did. After I had resolutely stayed in my room for the next two hours mentally daring anybody to further torment me, I emerged to find that nobody had even noticed I wasn't there and they were all ready to head to the registry office without me.

"Danny are you no even ready, look at you, get a move on" Dorothy said pushing me back into the room.

"What time are the cars getting here" I asked.

Dorothy laughed and said "Cars, what cars, we're all going on the subway up to Buchanan street and then bolt round to Martha street, if I canny walk in these heels you and Charlie will have to carry me, now come on there's less than an hour before we need to be there move move move."

"Ha ha, me and Charlie carry you, did you think Charlie has turned into a crane or something" I said escaping her clutches by ducking into my room attempting to undress and dress at the same time and consequently tripping over my own feet and banging my face on the corner of the bed.

So forty five minutes later we were standing outside Martha street registry office waiting for Elaine and her family to arrive, all of us, every single one of us was there dressed to the nines (Well for us anyway), and what a sight for sore eyes we must have been. Darlene and Dorothy had opted for the orange and lime leisure suits they had been modelling a few weeks before. Annie had on the outfit she had worn at her own wedding I think, or maybe it was the outfit my ma wore to her wedding. Donnie and Dunky had almost matching light coloured three piece suits on, with bell bottom trousers and matching waistcoats. They almost looked presentable if only Donnie hadn't spoiled it by wearing his nearly new Adidas trainers with his suit, Dunky thought that looked stupid so he opted for his black steel toe capped working boots, much more elegant I'm sure. Donnie had also actually got his hair curly permed, Dunky hadn't gone that far but they still looked like a couple of chancers.

The rest of us were clean enough I suppose but hardly the height of elegance both Charlie and I had black sandshoes on and Paul and the rest of the weans all had plastic sandals welded to their feet, but at least the various shirts shorts jackets and trousers we had on weren't torn (much). And thank god none of us had any of those horrible pageboy suits on, although the one Charlie wore to the previous wedding was considered for Paul, but it turned out it was a bit too big.

"Danny, how can they do a scramble here?" wee Paul asked me, as I craned my neck trying to see Past Darlene to find out if there was any sight of Elaine and her family.

"I don't know, what are you talking about?" I replied without paying much attention.

So Paul in his usual manner of communication punched me in the testicles and said "A scramble, you know what I mean, when the woman getting married throws all her change out of the window and all the weans scramble for it?, how can they do it here, it's a busy road, and when will they do it, when she gets here or after they're married and she's leaving, or will they do it when we get down to the conception in Govan"

Charlie thought the punch to the testicles was hilariously funny and lifted wee Paul's arm up as if he was a boxer, declaring him to be the winner by a knockout.

Darlene also laughed and said to wee Paul "It's a wedding reception you wee eejit, no a conception, a conception is a catholic thing, you do if you're a lassie when your about twelve, but you do get to wear a wedding dress so I suppose it's a wee bit like a reception right enough when you think about it maybe you're not really that stupid really."

I was in too much pain between my legs to properly take the pish out of Darlene for her stupidity in commenting on Pauls stupidity, anyway two taxies arrived and stopped right in front of us.

"Will you look at the state of that hat" Darlene said obviously referring to the hat that Elaine's sister was wearing that had more than a passing resemblance to a sombrero, with the utmost kindness it could possibly be described as a wide brimmed straw hat but in all honesty, it was a sombrero which somebody had brought back from Spain or something, and apart from that she was it was sat on top of what must have started out as a beehive hairdo, but was now more like a b-movie hairdo.

"Darlene, just shut up I won't tell you again, if you do anything to spoil Dunky's day< I won't forgive you now I mean it keep that mouth of yours shut" my Ma clearly wisnae in the mood for Darlene's nonsense, she looked all worried as well, first Dunky and Donnie, now her what's going on.

"Out of the second taxi emerged Elaine in a wedding dress several sizes too big for her and that wouldn't have been out of place on Princess Margaret.

"Danny go and find Dunky and Donnie tell them Elaine and her family are here to get a move on" Dorothy said pushing me in the back to hurry me along.

“Aye tell them the space ship has landed and the aliens are coming” Darlene couldn’t resist. The look my Ma gave her stopped any chance she had of enjoying her own joke.

Martha street registry office is a very big building with quite a few places to hide if you really want to, I stood just inside the entrance door at the bottom of a big flight of stairs, wondering where I could start looking when I spotted a sign for the toilets and guessed that would be as good a place as any to start looking for them, Charlie pushed into my back and said “You better move your arse they will all be in here in a minute”

It briefly entered my mind to punch him straight in the mouth but that probably wouldn’t have helped find Dunky. We both raced towards the toilet door which I reached just ahead of Charlie, pushing through with him right behind I immediately heard Dunky and Donnie having a loud conversation, not quite an argument but getting there, I put my hand out holding Charlie back from fully entering the toilet where the other two would see us.

“Who said I do, who made that fucking rule up, who said you have to get married just because you were too drunk to use a Johnny one night or didnae pull it out in time.” Dunky shouted belligerently into Donnie’s face, he must also have pushed Donnie because we heard what sounded like his back colliding with a cubicle door.

“My Ma, that’s who made that rule, why does my Ma get to make the rules up about my life, I don’t even want to get married, look at you you’re married and what did you get a crowd of screaming wee blonde weans and a woman that follows you about every minute of the day, you can hardly get moving for Annie, where are you going Donnie, where have you been Donnie, the weans need shoes Donnie, Mark’s got the cold Donnie don’t go out with Dunky the night, wee Maggie’s coming down with something just stay in the night.” Dunky sounded as if he was pacing up and down in front of the sinks and he wisnae happy.

"Well I don't want that, I want to go up the dancing every weekend and get a different bird every week, I don't want weans, I don't want a house of my own, I want to get rat arsed drunk on a Saturday morning or a Wednesday fucking morning if I feel like it, so why should I get married just because my ma says I have to, well I'm not, no fucking chance I'm just no doing in" he actually sounded as if he was close to tears.

"Are you finished" Donnie asked "well are you finished, if you are getting married because my Ma told you then you're a diddy, but you aren't are you, you're getting married because you don't have a choice, you got her pregnant you need to marry her, you did it, you do the right thing, what if you don't, what then she has the wean and somebody else brings it up for you, is that it, is that your big plan. Don't be an arse all your life, if it's your wean you get married, it is yours isn't it. Isn't it?" Donnie was getting angrier by the minute. By the sound of it Dunky was now getting pushed against the cubicle doors.

I was unsure whether to announce the arrival of the blushing bride or not, Charlie was in no such quandary, he roughly pushed past me, "You better make your mind up Dunky" he said as he walked fully into the toilet "Cinderella and the ugly sisters of just turned up in a black pumpkin"

Donnie put his arm round Dunky and pulled him close, kissing him on the cheek and said "Come on Dunky, head up big smile on your face, this disnae mean the end of your life, it just means you need to learn new rules, I still go out every weekend don't I, this disnae mean you have to be a monk, you just need to play the game that's all"

I couldn't resist neither could my mouth "Actually maybe you shouldn't be getting married if you prefer to stand about in toilets all day with an old man kissing you" I escaped by the skin of my teeth.

The wedding itself went reasonably well, my Ma seemed to just stare directly at Dunky the whole time, maybe expecting him to up sticks and run for the hills, I can't say that it would have been a major surprise if he had. But he didn't, to the casual observer, seeing him canoodling with the bride and flirting with the bridesmaids, it would probably have looked as if he was enjoying the whole process, Dunky is nothing if not charming, it's what he is good at. Donnie did his best to canoodle with bridesmaids but he found it difficult for two reasons, firstly he has no charm and doesn't know how to canoodle without groping and secondly, Annie was all over him like a rash, for most of the day she was closer to him than his vest.

The reception itself went the way of most Glasgow wedding receptions, pretty much everybody got drunk, pretty much all of the children at some point vomited pretty much all of the women felt abandoned by their men, and pretty much all of the men had a fight.

Darlene as per usual had all of the above and a little more. First of all she managed to get drunk twice, she was drunk within an hour of the reception beginning, thanks mostly to the half bottle of vodka she had down her knickers and the half bottle of Bacardi that her friend Sally Malcolm appeared with. You can imagine how happy I was to see her roll out of a taxi in and how much happier I was when, within five minutes, her and Darlene were standing screeching in a corner and pointing over at me laughing.

Darlene and Sally got so drunk so quickly that I overheard Dorothy telling my Ma that she had seen them both sitting beside a puddle of vomit in the ladies loo arguing about which one of them had been sick the most, Dorothy sent Tony to take them both back to her house for a wee sleep and a sober up and maybe even get changed out of their vomit covered clothes.

So when Darlene and Sally reappeared relatively sober at about eight o'clock that night it gave them a chance to get drunk again, and they did. If I tell you the full story of her very publicly having a stand up fist fight in the middle of the dance floor with her on/off boyfriend John Lawson which resulted in my Da again attempting to chase John down

Govan road, or about how she had a massive rammy in the toilet with the sombrero wearing bridesmaid, the you will be left with the impression that the day was all about Darlene, and I wouldn't want you thinking that it's enough that Darlene thought that.

There were lots of things happening that day that didn't involve Princess Darlene, there was a lovely touching moment when my Ma and Da danced a beautiful waltz and showed us what they must have been like in their twenties, my ma's eyes actually sparkled. And just as they finished the dance and the band started a new song my Da elegantly sat my Ma on a chair and in the same movement eased Elaine into his arms and danced across the floor with her, Elaine giggled like a schoolgirl throughout the twirling and gliding experience, my Da, very much like Dunky, could be an extremely charming and flirtatious man when in the limelight and under the influence.

I managed to just about avoid Sally Malcolm save one moment when we passed in the corridor between the ladies and gents toilets and she grabbed me and attempted a drunken kiss, I managed to hold her at arm's length until Annie came and rescued me with two well chosen words to Sally, the second one being "off"

Charlie managed to snag us some half pints of beer occasionally, from generous and inebriated uncles, which we consumed behind the curtains at the dark side of the stage the band was set up on.

Those half pints of lager were the main reason that I ended up under that stage with a bra less Shirley Anne, I won't go into detail, mainly because it was over so quick that there isn't much detail to go into. So there it was I became a man in amongst mouse shit and piles of discarded beer mats covered in many years of dust with a woman who was presumably semi oblivious to who I was, for all that I did enjoy it.

Printed in Great Britain
by Amazon